Breathe

One woman's journey

to save her husband and herself

By: Barbara L. Thornbury

Dedicated to all the caretakers of the world.

You are the true heroes of the story.

Acknowledgements

How do you thank an entire nation of friends and family? Without the love and support of everyone constantly telling me to publish, this book would not have become a reality. To all who have supported me, patiently awaiting this book, a huge thank you.

To **Susan Price**, my first great editor, you put me on my feet and gave me the courage to put this story into some sort of semblance of a book. I cannot thank you enough for helping me to get started.

To **Sarah Cripe**, my second great editor, for dusting me off, turning me in the right direction and setting me straight again. I cannot thank you enough for getting me going again.

To **Penny Thrawl**, you saved me from hours and hours of editing that I was dreading. I cannot thank you enough for keeping me from losing my mind that day when I was woman on the edge.

To **Hannah Rodriguez**, what a talented, young woman you are and my third great editor. I cannot thank you enough, for digging me out of the "writers block black hole" when I became stuck. This book is an actual book because of your amazing talents.

To **Jessica van Kuyk**, your artistic talent with a camera always inspires me and the book cover is perfect. I cannot thank you enough for putting up with all my requests for changes in the attempt to capture in a photograph, what is felt in my heart.

To **Brad Thornbury**, thanks for choosing me all those years ago and for not leaving me alone when the darkness descended. It was a wild ride, but let's not go through it again, okay?

To **My Readers**, I don't know you yet, but my deepest gratitude to all of you for your interest in my writing. I am humbled to think that you are willing to take a chance on me.

Breathe

Prologue

At the sound of his voice, I turn. "Hey, come feel this," my husband says as I rush around the kitchen. My husband of 24 years has his hand in his pocket, touching himself. "Are you out of your mind? The kids will be home any minute, I have cookies in the oven and I'm running late for my meeting," I fume. I'm annoyed that he wants to fool around in our kitchen at 3:30 in the afternoon. I'm busy and he's not helping.

"No, it's not that. It's this bump in my leg. Do you think it's scar tissue from that basketball injury, or could it be serious?"

My blood runs cold, the cookies burn, and I fight back a wave of fear. My heart starts to race uncontrollably. What if it's cancer?

Week 1: When Cancer Comes A-Calling

Day 1: After recovering from hearing the diagnosis that my husband has cancer, we survived a whirlwind week filled with tests, scans, and doctor appointments. Now therapy begins, a journey taken through radiation, chemotherapy, and surgery. It begins today and my husband has already left for the hospital in the city. I'm thinking that given his aversion to needles, having the PICC line put in just may be the worst part of this whole journey for him.

I told a friend this weekend that my theory on life is this: Each morning we wake up and pick up the backpack that God has given us and asks that we carry each day. Some of us are blessed with just feathers and flowers in their backpack. Others, like myself, carry a heavy pack filled with bricks. It is not for us to question why God chooses some of us for the brick-filled packs. It is enough just to know that He has given those of us enough muscle to shoulder the brick-filled packs. So we carry them, so others won't have to. I just have to keep reminding myself that I am strong enough to carry this brick-filled backpack.

My hope is that one day, I'll wake up to find a backpack filled with feathers and flowers.

It just won't be today.

Day 2: Chemotherapy started today. I had to drive my husband down into the city and drop him off for treatment, then come back home and get the boys to school. As I sat stopped on the expressway, I pondered once again, "How is it that not one person on earth is smart enough to figure out the traffic problems in Chicago?" Thankfully, the massive rainstorm, while making visibility near zero, washed our car for free.

I ran some errands in between carpools. Because I was forced to haul our groceries from over on Main Street through the downpour, my hair also got a free rinse. As if dealing with cancer isn't bad enough, our city decided now was a good time to tear up our street for the third time in fifteen years and it's currently impassable. This is a total tear out, with nothing but a mushy mess of gravel and sand left for us to walk on to get downtown. While I was trudging through the rain with water soaked boxes of cereal and pasta, the thought that had been scratching at the back of my brain finally bloomed.

"What if my husband needs an ambulance and I have to call 911? What do they do when they don't have a road to drive on?" Somehow this segued into "I wonder how my husband is doing on this first day of chemotherapy?" Which then led me to feeling guilty about being at home, slogging through the rain with a squashed, damp, box of Cap'n Crunch under one arm and a stack of Oreo packages under the other, instead of being with him. With each step, my guilt increased, as I beat myself up for my lack of support.

What had I been thinking not finding someone to run carpool for me, get groceries, feed the boys, help them with their homework, and make sure they were settled for the day so that I could sit with my husband while the vile poison dripped into his arm?

As the rain poured down on me, Cap'n Crunch became Cap'n Mush and I dropped the Oreo's into a muddy puddle in the middle of the road. As I stopped to retrieve the Oreo's, I realized the answer to that question was that I had tried my best on this first day of treatment to balance being a wife with being a mother. Although I might have gotten the balance too one-sided, at least my husband was getting chemotherapy and my sons were in school.

I continued the walk home, deciding that the Cap'n Mush was only going as far as the garbage can and that we would just have to have Oreo's for breakfast tomorrow. That was assuming that there would still be any left. I was planning on having them for lunch, despite having had cookies for breakfast. Let's face it, guilt is best served with a tall, cold glass of milk, and a baked circle of deliciousness.

Day 3: The path through Hell that cancer patients must walk is not a new path for me as a caregiver, but rather, a worn, dusty familiar road, well-trodden over the past 20 years. Having lost my best friend to breast cancer while we were both in our thirties, I was thrown into the world of chaos and pain that cancer creates. Still, I remained at a distance as she traveled that path mainly with her family.

Towards the end of her life, my own mother was diagnosed with two forms of cancer and I was immediately flung into a lower ring of Hell that only daughters can walk through when their mothers become ill.

So why was I surprised yesterday when the old chemo sign posts popped up; Blue Day, Rainbow Riot, and Chemo Fog? Was it that I had thought this time would be different? Or was it that I had hoped for just one more good day before the path took us down to another lower level of Hell?

Today is a new day, one day closer to the end of treatment and that beautiful, shiny town called Remission. I'll hang on to Winston Churchill's musing, "when going through Hell, keep walking," as my husband and I walk this dusty path together. The backpack feels heavier today, or maybe I'm just a little more fatigued. I need to suck it up though. I know it's going to get worse before this gets better.

Day 5: The high point of the day came when I was driving to the hospital this afternoon and there was a massive traffic jam on the expressway. What was the cause you ask? Why, a man on the side of the road, on his hands and knees, trying to fix a flat tire.

Why would that slow down traffic you ask? Why, because his pants were down around his knees and he was bare ass naked, fixing the flat. I was sorry that I didn't own a cell phone. Otherwise, there would have been a picture to post on social media with some clever tag like, "Motorist gets left BEHIND in traffic jam due to flat."

That was the high point of the day.

The low point was that the word defining Day 5 was 'vomit'. Vomit spraying on the bedroom floor as the bathroom was too far away. Little bits of white rice, like maggots creeping down the wall in search of a new host vomit. Ropy, stringy, mucus of brown sticky goo skidding across the floor vomit. Vomit on the bedspread, vomit on the nightstand, vomit, vomit, vomit.

Vomit in great, gushing geysers, never-ending. Leaving my husband weak, shaky, and lying in a fetal position on the cold, tile floor of the bathroom where the episode finally drew to an end. I was also left weak and shaky from my inability to help him.

This was the Rainbow Riot my mother and I would talk about when she went through chemotherapy. How, no matter what went in, a mixture of colors would come back up; creating a Rainbow Riot of mysterious colors and textures. I had forgotten about this. Or maybe I had hoped that we would somehow avoid this level of vomiting. My denial had blinded me to the truths that I know exist about chemotherapy. A reality check in the form of a vomit mural on the bedroom wall, floor, and furniture brought all this back into my consciousness.

I can't wait until the Chemo Fog drifts in now. That's such a treat for everyone. Nothing like that strange, fogged mind, with almost no short-term memory, to keep us all on our toes.

After the IV fluids are delivered tonight I'm going to go on a big sleep. Hopefully, tomorrow will be vomit-free.

Day 5: The *real* Day 5, not like yesterday, when it was really Day 4. Looks like Chemo Fog has settled into our home after all and is affecting my brain too. Oh boy.

Right now our street is closed for construction. It's been reduced to gravel and sand with no traffic being allowed through. There are no street lights either, this being a small town with a limited budget. So when the IV fluids came last night around 9:30, the delivery people called from the church down the street on the corner. They said they were on a tight schedule and, "Could I come down and get the supplies?"

In my pajamas, in the pitch black, I ran down to the church. Slipping and sliding through the gravel and sand, it felt like an eternity passed before I reached them. Overweight, out of shape, asthmatic, exhausted, this was not how I had envisioned the endless day of vomit to end.

After I had signed the approximately seven hundred release forms, I then faced the challenge of carrying an IV pole and two heavy bags of supplies back to my home. If I thought running through the quicksand-like sludge was a treat on the way down to the church, the return journey with supplies in hand was almost impossible.

I got only a block away from home and had to stop. Actually, I collapsed, falling to my knees right there in the middle of the street in the mud, muck, and gravel.

Now, I try to put a positive spin on the crap that seems to happen to me all the time. I decided to stay there and thank God for the good things until my breathing subsided and I could go on. Even if I had to sit there all night, digging deep to find a positive twist, I was going to find something to be thankful for. What came to me was a memory of when my son was five years old.

For Thanksgiving that year, the kids in kindergarten were given paper feathers for a turkey they were decorating. The teacher asked them to write what they're thankful for on each feather. Mom, dad, sister, brother, grandparents, the usual, pretty predictable answers were given. Not my son though. He wrote: Tigers, penguins, and giraffes. When asked why, he replied, "Everyone always forgets them, but we need to be thankful for them too."

So last night, I thanked God for tigers, penguins, and giraffes. For cookies for breakfast, asphalt streets that are well lit, and 20-year-old Garfield pajamas that still fit. For at-home IV poles, heavy-duty sleeping meds, and the cold weather front that has arrived. For the strength that I have been given to get through each day. Then I continued my walk home, dragging the supplies behind me. When I finally entered our house, I realized I had lost a slipper either on the way to the church or on the way back. I hoped a chipmunk or mouse found it and used it for a home. I wasn't going back out there to find it. Let's face it, it was ugly anyway.

Day 6: It's funny how, at these darkest of hours, I don't even need to send up a prayer to God for Him to hear my thoughts. As I sat on the toilet this morning, I pondered if I would get to a point in this journey where we would run out of toilet paper because I had quite simply forgotten to purchase some. As someone who has run businesses, government, and households, I'm now reduced to living in the immediate moment by just trying to get through each day. Even if that means surviving without toilet paper or toothpaste.

But, God heard my troubled thoughts and hours later, when I had finally found time to take a shower, a friend stopped by with TOILET PAPER, and groceries!!! Finding these treasures sitting in my kitchen when I came down the stairs, my hair still dripping wet, felt like winning the lottery.

So far, today has gone better than the first 5 days. The scopolamine patch, which is supposed to control the vomiting, seems to be giving my husband some much needed relief and he's able to concentrate on his Fantasy Football team.

I am forever thankful for the amazing friends and family we have, and today I say thank you to God for hummingbirds, good people, zebra's, blue sunny skies, tomato plants, toilet paper, and scopolamine patches.

Day 7: I was reminded of something that happened in high school, so very long ago...

Junior year, my communications teacher would periodically take breaks from our daily assignments of persuasive speeches and random arguments to ask us pointed questions. They were meant to get our 17 year-old brains thinking about something other than what we were going to wear the next day or who Johnny Goodlooking was going to ask to the next formal dance.

One day, she asked the question, "Is the pitcher half empty or half-full?" Now, many interpret this to be a measure of pessimism or optimism, but for me, this is a question of honesty. For who would be so bold to answer half-full in a room full of teen aged angst-filled high school students?

When it came time for my answer, I looked my teacher straight in the eye and gave my honest reply, "Who cares? I'm just glad I have a pitcher each day." Three things happened simultaneously: she got misty eyed, someone from the back of the class shouted, "What the hell does that mean?!?" and Johnny Goodlooking blew air into the crook of his arm, firing off a fart sound that caused every girl in the class to rethink whether they would say yes to him if they were deemed worthy of a request from him about prom.

Into this melee, I replied, "It's simple, really. If I have a pitcher, I can collect rain water if I'm thirsty. I can collect berries if I'm hungry. I can collect shells on the beach. I can do thousands of things, but I must have the pitcher to do them."

Today is Day 7 and the pitcher is half-empty. We are out of cookies so I didn't know what to eat for breakfast. The car had a flat tire, making us late again. Traffic on the interstate was horrendous. Construction outside my house was making my head throb. My son was not feeling well. My husband has cancer.

Today is Day 7 and the pitcher is half-full. We have toilet paper. One week of radiation and chemotherapy are over. The blue sky was incredible today. I own a car. I own a house. We're being fed incredibly well by our family and friends. My son will get over this intestinal bug soon.

...and in 10 more weeks, my husband is going to be just fine and we will be throwing a massive party. Everyone will bring an empty pitcher, and then we're going to fill them all up with margaritas and celebrate. It's really just that simple.

I might even invite Johnny Goodlooking to the party. I've heard he sometimes gets Saturday evenings off over at the penitentiary for good behavior.

Week 2: Can Coffee Be Administered Intravenously?

Day 8: My husband had a rough night, so I woke at 5:00 AM with that hangover feeling you get from lack of sleep. I leaned over and picked up my proverbial backpack to start the day, and it felt heavier than it has ever felt before. I felt crushed under the weight and worried that I wouldn't be able to continue on this journey. Somehow though, I made it into the kitchen.

I started the coffee, fed the dog and cat, and banged on the coffee pot again to try to speed it up.

While it was churning and burning, I prepped the heparin flush materials for my husband's port cleaning. I realized today was Tuesday, and therefore, also dressing changing day. So, I grabbed the bag of supplies.

When removing the gauze package, I noticed that it had the following stamped on it:

"Expires October 2014"

It might have been lack of sleep, or lack of coffee, or both, but I immediately started pondering the significance of this in my life.

If we have a traumatic injury that requires gauze in November 2014, can I use the expired stuff? What if we don't use the gauze prior to November 2014, thus wasting valuable resources? Should I use it, say, in September 2014 for drying dishes, so that I won't feel like I've wasted anything? Once I've used it for drying dishes, can it be washed and used again, maybe to dry off the dog's feet?

Most importantly, why the HELL does gauze have an expiration date?!?!

The barfing up of a large clot of thick coffee into the pot broke my reverie and as I took the first sip, I realized that humor is the best way to start the day. Of course, I had to chew the coffee because the coffee pot expired in June of 2003 and I was still using it.

Day 9: I woke late and started the day without drinking any coffee. I would like to think that I'm not addicted to coffee and that I could walk away from the daily dose anytime. But, this morning I walked into a pole hanging in our basement, gashing my head and bringing stars to my vision so, I'm thinking the coffee may just be like an insurance premium. You pay it and somehow never have any reason to make a claim, but the moment you let your insurance lapse, that's when the basement floods, the kitchen catches on fire, and the roof collapses. Best to drink the coffee, I think.

After the head wound incident, I walked over to Main Street to retrieve my car to run carpool and get my son. Walking up to the car, I thought I saw something hanging down underneath. I lay down flat and squeezed up under the car. It turned out to be nothing, so I got up and wiped the grease on my pants, only to realize, it was 10:00 in the morning, and I was still wearing my pajamas.

Now, my first thought was, "How the hell did I forget to get dressed this morning?" My second thought was, "Do I run home and change, or run carpool in my pajamas?" My third thought was, "If I didn't shower today, did I at least brush my teeth?" My fourth thought was, "Do

I care that I'm in front of the neighbor's house in my pajamas?"

Turns out, I don't care that I'm running around my neighborhood in faded Garfield the Cat pajama pants and an old, coffee stained t-shirt that my husband wore to play basketball back in 1984. I got in the car, turned the car on, and I'm not making this up, "Bringing Sexy Back" by Justin Timberlake was playing on the radio.

Hot damn! I felt good!

Day 10: The medical insurance merry-go-round started today. The first Explanation of Benefits arrived with a weird code next to the CT scan saying it was not covered. When I looked up the code, it said:

"We do not cover this service for the diagnosis reported"

So, we needed the CT to discover my husband's cancer, but they don't cover the CT scan so we shouldn't have gotten it done? I called the insurance company and spent a long, torturous half hour with someone halfway across the globe as we haggled over coverage for the scan. I almost gave up at one point in the negotiations when the agent said in broken English, "Don't shoot at the messenger, please," as if my frustration at his misunderstanding of language were painful bullets shot into his heart. We finally agreed that the scan would be recoded and resubmitted. If nothing else, it bought me some time.

At the end of the conversation I told him the next time I would use Tarot cards and self-hypnosis for the diagnosis, as those were probably covered. He told me I was probably right, but to make sure I had the correct code.

It felt really, really good tonight to take this overburdened, bulging back-pack off and throw it on the bedroom floor.

Day 11: Earlier this week we had a mishap with the car, so we were running late to treatment. As is always the case, traffic that day was worse than ever, making us late and increasing my stress level.

Two miles from the hospital, with my husband not feeling well, he said he needed to be at the hospital NOW. We decided that, rather than snake crawl along the interstate, we'd get off onto the frontage road that runs parallel to it.

Once on the frontage road, it was like some weird scene shift in a horror movie. Garbage everywhere, graffiti, broken down cars, we passed block after block of sadness and decay. I accelerated, not caring if we were pulled over by the police, half hoping that we would be so they could escort us out of this poorly written novel about death and decay into which we'd been thrust.

We passed a playground with the garbage heaped everywhere and I thought, "What parent in their right mind would take their children to such a dismal, decrepit garbage pit to play in?" I wondered why the city didn't just tear the playground out and leave it as an empty city block instead. As we slowly drove past, I realized that the garbage was moving.

The reality of what I was truly seeing slammed into me. These were not piles of garbage, these were human beings. These were people who live here, out on the street, with nowhere to go. This was not some run-down playground that was in desperate need of a few trash collectors. No, this was an outdoor home for a vast number of societies forgotten.

I heard a droning in the van, "My God, My God, My God"....over and over and over. I turned to look at my husband and discovered that the chanting was coming from me, not him.

The mantra coming from my husband was a sub-human moaning and I started to panic. We needed to be at the hospital NOW. We needed to be out of this horror story NOW. We needed to find our way back to normal NOW. We needed this day to be over NOW.

And it was.

Just like that, the hospital loomed up in front of us and I pulled up to the clean, white, sparkling curb and let my husband out. Reality shifted back to what I knew as our normal and time went on.

I realized, in that moment, that we are only put on this earth for one purpose: to care for our fellow man. If we are not doing that, then we have failed in our purpose. We have failed as a society.

I also realized, that no matter how heavy my backpack is, there are those among us whose burden is greater. Others who have fallen under the weight of their overloaded backpacks and desperately need someone's help to get back up on their feet.

Tomorrow is a new opportunity for us to take care of one another. Tomorrow is a new opportunity for all of us to get it right. Tomorrow is a new opportunity.

Day 12: Yesterday was a good day for my husband. He was able to drive himself to radiation, then go into work afterwards. He drank coffee for the first time in eleven days and never once vomited. He showered with a plastic sleeve on his arm, instead of taking a bath and felt more like himself again. He wore a pair of jeans and a button-down shirt, instead of sweat pants and a baggy shirt, necessary during treatment. We had a lovely dinner with a dear friend as if everything was back to how our lives used to be.

It all felt so normal.

Yesterday was a good day for me too. When my son was driving me to the grocery store, he misjudged the turn and instead of braking, accelerated over a concrete curb. We were actually airborne for a bit, eventually coming to a stop on the edge of a retention pond near the parking lot. I swallowed my terror and a primal scream of "YEE-HAW!" instead responding with, "bit fast going into that turn, huh?" After an hour of shopping, my hands were still shaking, but at least we had a new week's supply of cookies and milk.

Later in the day, the dog ran away twice because the gate was open. I was forced to run around the neighborhood screaming her name, while muttering under my breath "Why do we have a dog?" like some crazy old lady. I was wearing my Garfield the Cat pajama pants again. This time with a shirt that I first wore during my disco phase decades ago, so the neighbors didn't think anything of it. They've seen this routine too many times in the past to have it even register in their minds.

I went to do a load of laundry and found someone (who I doubt will ever claim responsibility) had left a package of chewing gum, three sharpie markers and a half-eaten granola bar in their pants pockets. That all of this had made its way through the wash cycle, through the dryer cycle marked "Hot Damn!" by the last repairman and into a basket without my noticing, probably should have been partly my responsibility. The resulting mosaic on the inside of the dryer was actually a beautiful work of art, one I hope the repairman appreciates when he comes to clean out the barrel.

While opening the lid on a can of paint, I stabbed myself with the screwdriver. As this is a commonplace event in my life, I didn't even realize I was cut and bleeding, until I spilled paint onto the shredded finger and it burned like mad. When I reached for a rag to staunch the bleeding, I knocked over the paint can onto the garage floor. My response was to yell an expletive, which is what

I scream when the dog runs away, so she came running moments after the curse word left my lips. The dog persisted on running around the garage in the paint, quickly transforming the garage floor into a comical CSI version of a paint can homicide. As I grabbed the dog to prevent her from running into the house, I heard a voice speak my name and turned to see my neighbor standing in the driveway. I asked him what he had said and he replied, "I said, do you need help?"

Hmmm, that's an interesting question. Help with the paint, the dog, the bleeding, shredded finger? Or help getting to a local psychoanalyst for some much needed therapy?

This is my life. It all felt so normal.

Yesterday, was a very, very, very good day.

Day 13: Last night, as I was waiting on hold with the mortgage company and trying to balance the checkbook at the same time, it started to rain. I sent a silent prayer of thanks to God since I had planted a few mums earlier in the day and had forgotten to water them.

From somewhere in the house my husband yelled that two of our toilets were leaking and the dining room ceiling was showing signs of water damage. While pondering if I had the energy or clarity of thought to deal with the leaking toilets, I sneezed uncontrollably a dozen times and dived for my inhaler. Since I was still on hold with the mortgage company, I was subjected to the Muzak droning in my ear, turning my brain to pudding. I wondered if this day would ever end.

As I was considering hanging up and losing the twenty minutes of my life I had just spent on hold, my son came into the office to inform me that he needed thirty-three bottles of Gatorade for school tomorrow. The store was closing in fifteen minutes, so we needed to leave now through a torrential downpour.

Our car was still parked on Main Street because our road was still closed. Apparently, the life of a construction project is counted, not in people time, but dog days. We were told it would take a week, but it is almost day twenty of the project. I'm guessing we have another twenty-nine dog days of construction to go.

So, we walked through the rain and the dark to our car, circumventing the raging river of muck and mire, surging down the street. Since it was late, I decided not to change out of my pajamas on the premise that I wouldn't run into anyone I know at the store. I should have remembered this invokes one of those theorems of life. Such as; "On bad hair days you are guaranteed to run into a past lover" or "Being late by fifteen minutes so you could apply makeup is better than arriving on time, with no makeup, and your friend's child announcing that Shrek has arrived." So why did I forget the most important life theorem? "When leaving the house on a rainy night in Garfield the Cat pajama pants with a t-shirt from the 90's that proclaims your love for Duran, Duran, to buy a cartful of energy drinks at the store, don't be surprised if someone with a phone snaps your picture."

I cursed the rain. I cursed cell phones. I cursed energy drinks and English teachers who award points to students who bring food to class.

I realize that some people think I make this stuff up; signs of a creative mind with too little sleep and too little human contact. Too much time spent in old, faded pajamas, in a home under supplied with toilet paper.

The truth is though, that this is my life. The toilets were leaking. One of which was threatening to collapse the entire dining room ceiling. I was damp and coughing in line at the store last night with three cases of sport drinks and a teenager with a bad attitude.

And a long time ago, I accepted that this is my life. I realized that if you walk through life with grace, accept all that you are given and put a positive spin on it, then each and every day is going to be okay.

So, I really was thankful for the rain. For my hair will be nice and shiny in the morning from the rain rinsing it.

I'm thankful that the cat shredded all the important documents on my desk while we were gone, because now I don't need to pay those bills until next month when the late notices arrive.

I'm thankful for this cold, because that's all it is. I'll be better in a few days and I get to justify going to bed early tonight.

I'm thankful for this crazy life that is mine, because God chose it for me.

Day 14: If rabies is a disease that is fearful of liquids, then cancer is a disease in love with them.

Cancer obsesses with liquids.

"Honey, just now when you vomited, would you say that it was 8 ounces or 12 ounces? Were your meds in there? Don't flush, I need to analyze and document."

"When you got up at 1:48 a.m. to urinate, was it clear, yellow or orange? How much did you output? What do you mean you didn't turn on the light? How am I supposed to document the pee if you are viewing it with night-crusted eyes in the dark?"

To IV or not to IV, that's the question that keeps me up at night, trying to balance liquids in with liquids out.

Cancer's obsession with liquids is about washing your hands to the point that they bleed. Then washing them even more because now you're an even bigger risk to the patient. Wiping down surfaces and pondering how you can flush the toilet without actually touching the handle. Bleach and Febreze become the perfumes of choice, bypassing the Clinique "Happy" bottle each morning because the smell is too much for anyone in chemotherapy.

Cancer reduces your shopping experience to buying only liquids. All the chicken noodle soup, one of every pudding flavor, and wondering if the one tea missing from the cabinet (the PMS Blend) is the undiscovered miracle tea for curing cancer, and should you buy it to add to the 204 other tea boxes that you have amassed at home. Chewing becomes a thing of the past.

If there is one liquid cancer loves above all others, it's the tears shed during moments of weakness. Driving through traffic on the interstate, the bread aisle at the store, sitting on a toilet at the hospital, tears spring forth unbidden, unwanted at the most inopportune time. It's as if the tears are a purging of the soul, a release of all the fear, anger, rage, disgust, and failure that builds as the battle with cancer rages on. This is the liquid that feeds cancer, nurtures it. Our tears give strength to cancer as they come in our moments of exhaustion and weakness.

It's the one liquid I'm ready to be done with.

Yes, that smell was of coffee at 2:56 a.m. at our house. I couldn't sleep this night, my mind racing back through the past toward the last moments of my mother's life. How my mother loved coffee, loved having friends over for a cup of dark, thick brew, something wonderful she had baked that morning and gossip from the neighborhood. How toward the end, when cancer had invaded every corner of her body, the one thing she still requested was her early morning cup of coffee.

Coffee is another liquid that is essential when cancer comes to visit, as exhaustion is a common companion. It's one of the few things we're still chewing at our home because I brew it the way my mom did, thick and rich. I brew it that way, especially on this day, which would have been her 77th birthday.

That is, if cancer hadn't come and taken her away.

Week 3: If Laughter Is The Best Medicine, Why Isn't It Sold At The Pharmacy?

Day 15: While sitting at the family reunion last night, I looked over to check on my husband, and my first thought was, "If given a box of 128 Crayola's, what color would I choose to match his face? Canary yellow? Inchworm green? Manatee grey?" This was followed by, "Do I take him home and call the doctor or just save time and go to the local emergency room?" We left in a flurried haste, leaving amid hasty good-byes and forgotten personal belongings. I didn't care; it was family after all.

By the time we got home, he was spiking a fever. Not entirely something you have to freak out about with cancer patients; let's face it, white blood cells, red blood cells, platelets, any or all, can plummet and cause a spiky fever. But so can infection, so phone calls were made, and the doctor sent me to a twenty-four hour pharmacy in the next town over.

When I got there, a woman with a cane and disheveled hair was at the counter, shrieking and shaking slightly. She raged on about NEEDING the Oxycontin TONIGHT and that her insurance company didn't UNDERSTAND that there were thirty-one days last month and that's why she's here ten days early, NOT because she's been misusing the Oxy. I tried to assimilate this, realized I couldn't and focused instead on the music flooding down from the overhead speakers.

It was Journey, "Don't Stop Believing", and I felt a weird disconnect with reality. "Don't Stop Believing?" Really? In the pharmacy at 11:34PM? Was Muzak a thing of the past? Was there significance to this song? Don't Stop Believing that this night will never end? Don't Stop Believing that cancer will soon be gone from our home? Don't Stop Believing that the prescription will actually be filled in the next five minutes and you can finally go home?

As I was trying to formulate a theory on this, Little River Band's "Cool Change" came on and I was called up to the counter. I thought about asking the pharmacist about the music (was it meant to be some sort of subliminal pick-me-up?) but Ms. I'm-Addicted-To-Oxycontin was still raging on about NEEDING her pain meds, so I merely gave the pharmacy technician my husband's name.

She responded that there was nothing for him. "Perhaps it hasn't been filled?" I said. Fifteen minutes passed as phone calls were made to the doctor's answering service and Ms. Just-Give-Me-The-Oxycontin-and-No-One-Will-Get-Hurt raged on and on. An hour passed. Eventually, Ms. Oxycontin-Is-My Personal-Friend slumped over in a chair and quickly fell into a deep sleep. Someone enquired of the pharmacist whether there was someone that could be called to help the sleeping addict and he quickly replied that this tableau was played out, each and every night for a full week each month prior to her prescription being refilled. She would eventually wake and quietly leave the pharmacy, only to return and rage the following evening until the day when she could leave with a full bottle of medication.

During this hour-long adventure, more phone calls were made to my husband's doctor and I was subjected to a musical medley that spanned forty years of rock and roll, jazz, hip hop, and kid's songs. I started to formulate a plan in my mind. If Queen's "Another One Bites the Dust" came on, I would take this as a sign to hurt someone. As I was recognizing that my exhaustion was coloring my ability to make good decisions, I decided it was best to go home and wait for them to call me back after everything was straightened out. Despite it being almost 1 a.m., I told the pharmacist to ring the house when the medications were finally ready to be picked up.

I decided on the way home that surely that was the worst thing to have to listen to ever. The crazy mixed 80's songs peppered by Ms. Oxycontin-For-Breakfast yelling about her NEEDS. I just wanted the peace of my home to calm my nerves. Hopefully, I would be returning to the pharmacy soon, so I figured a quick check on my husband was in order before I put the coffee pot on the "Sludge Setting".

The first thing that hit me when I opened the bedroom door was the temperature in the room. Hot, stuffy, and what my dad would have described as "close".

The second thing that hit me caused my bones to dissolve, my muscles to melt, my entire being to drain away through the floorboards, because I was oh so wrong about the music at the pharmacy. It wasn't the worst thing to listen to, in fact, it was heavenly. This, this, was the worst sound on the planet. This horrible moaning, surfacing from somewhere deep within my husband, this was the worst sound to ever hit my eardrums. He was not well and without the medications, I was powerless to help him.

Standing there, unsure of what to do to help him, the phone rang and I stumbled toward it. It was the doctor.

The pharmacy had screwed up and she was livid. She was sorry that it was now almost 2:15 a.m. and I would have to go back to the 24-hour pharmacy. She was sorry, but she wanted those medications in my husband as soon as possible, so back I would need to go. She told me she hoped the rest of the night would go better. I wanted to tell her the night was almost over, dawn a few hours away. I wanted to tell her I couldn't do this anymore, that we needed a vacation from cancer, if only for a week. I wanted to tell her it couldn't possibly get any worse, but I knew, once spoken, those words would somehow cause things to get worse, so I said nothing.

An hour later, everything was back to normal. My husband was sleeping peacefully, the fever crushed by medication, snoring ever so slightly. I realized this was the music that I sought so fervently for the last few hours. It meant the pain had abated, the fever was down. I fell asleep listening to this amazing and beautiful song of life being snored out, note-by-note, right next to me.

Day 16: Almost 20 years ago, a woman in town was critically injured, and although she could walk around, she could do nothing within her home. As president of the local women's group back then, I was called and mobilized a meal schedule, carpool, and help for her.

On my night to deliver a home-cooked meal for her, I left work early, cooked, then went over to her home before 5:00 p.m. so her family could eat on time.

When I got there, I asked her how she was doing and if there was anything else she needed of me before I left. She thanked me for dinner, then said, "Could you scrub my kitchen floor before you leave?"

Now, I worked full time, had a 2-year-old daughter, was president of the women's group, and did outside volunteer work for various agencies. I was a busy person. I was also eight months pregnant and getting down on my hands and knees to scrub a floor took a monumental reserve of energy I didn't think I had.

I thought the woman had lost her mind. Did she really expect me to get down on that floor and scrub it? Wasn't it enough that we were all giving our time and talents to keep her family fed and delivered on time to various schools and scouting events? Couldn't she just let her kitchen floor go for a few weeks?

I looked at her face and saw utter exhaustion. I saw desperation. I saw sadness and pain. I saw defeat. I also saw that she wanted her kitchen floor clean.

So, I scrubbed her floor. I scrubbed her cabinets. Then I embraced her before I left, for she had given me the most amazing gift, and I wasn't sure if I could ever repay her. She had opened my eyes to the reality of sickness and injury; she had shown me that sometimes that which is most important is just doing the normal, everyday chores. That when we pursue the ordinary each day, we're given the extraordinary, and somehow it makes us feel human again.

I don't need anyone to stop by and scrub my floors. My motto has always been, "My house was clean yesterday, I'm so sorry you missed it," and really, why change what works for us just because of a little cancer?

No, my point in all of this is, cherish the ordinary, embrace the average, celebrate the humdrum steady beat that goes on under the surface. That's the pace we need to follow each day.

Not this crazy techno-treadmill that society has placed us on.

Day 17: There are benefits to my husband having cancer.

His hair will fall out soon and we'll be able to save $1.99 per month on shampoo.

We've discussed what to do with this windfall. Treat ourselves to a third of a cup of coffee at a coffee shop? Search parking lots for a lost penny, so we both could have something off the dollar menu at McDonald's? Purchase matching knit caps at the Dollar Store? Too many possibilities to consider.

Another benefit is when solicitors call our home.

"HELLO! This is HANK from Ameri-Pharm Industries! Have I got a deal for you on Viagra right now!"

"Oh HANK, thank goodness you called during our dinner time. My husband has cancer and he's probably going to be sick and nauseous in the next half hour, so calling during dinner was perfect! I was just telling my husband the other day while all his hair was falling out, I said, honey, you need to get that Viagra stuff for baldness and rub it all over your head. That will make your hair grow back!"

"Hello, Hank, are you there?"

One of the best benefits is, you get a professional nurse to come to your home to help with the infusion stuff that you personally are not trained on and know nothing about.

"Hi! This is Holly with Happy Home Health Happenings! What does your husband need this weekend?"

"IV fluids and a dressing change."

"Oh, I'm not trained for dressing changes. Is IV fluids like hydration or something?"

"Ummm, …do you know Hank?"

If the two choices in life are to laugh at yourself and your situation, or crawl into a corner and cry, then choose laughter every time. It makes the days more interesting and the backpack a little bit lighter.

Day 18: I met my husband thirty-one years ago in high school. Somehow, over the past three decades together, life fell into a comfortable routine. Each morning it felt like we were getting into a Mercedes, leather seats welcoming us, engine softly purring like a cat sleeping in sunlight. We would take turns driving through the day, and retire the car at night with little or no worries about tomorrow. The routine was easy, calming in the repetitiveness of it all.

Then one day, cancer drove up in an old clunker, with a blown transmission, noisy exhaust, and no windshield wipers.

"Get in," cancer said, and we knew we had no choice.

Each day, we rise and trudge wearily to the junker, dreading the ride ahead. Cancer always drives, each and every day, and we are never allowed control of that car.

The engine squeals, shrieks, moans and bellows its way through the drive. With no shocks or struts, we feel every hole in the road, the ride a jarring, jangling, torturous ride. We take every turn desperately hanging onto one another.

With no wipers, the windshield is a foggy, dark mess, and we cannot see the road ahead of us. For this, we are actually grateful.

We return from this exhausting journey each day, sore, broken, depleted, diminished. We will rise the next morning, still exhausted, but will make the trip again. We must.

In a few weeks, the metaphorical Mercedes will be returned to us and cancer will drive off in a cloud of black smoke, "Highway to Hell" by AC/DC blasting from the speakers. We will continue our life's journey in the Mercedes, but will forever be checking the rear-view mirror for that hated junker, driven by that hideous monster, cancer.

I just hope that, at some point in my life, that hateful junker drives off a cliff somewhere, and no one ever has to take this ride through Hell ever again.

Day 19: It's good to have my husband back home and to be back in our "new normal" routine.

Yesterday was not good. Twenty hours of not good. But here's what happened, the story that needs to be told.

Wednesday morning, my husband woke up spewing like Old Faithful and none of the medications were helping. It was decided that I would take him to radiation anyway, and we would see what the doctor said, after his treatment.

I was waiting in the reception room as a woman came in and sat close to me.

She was not well. She was alone. She started to weep. A quiet, gentle sobbing, but she was crying, alone, all the same. It started pulling bits and pieces of my heart off, so I went over to her. Was there something I could get for her? Anything I could do?

She squeezed my hand. Here was someone, lost alone in the pain and sickness, unable to speak she was crying so hard by then. I was utterly at a loss for words. I didn't know how to help her.

While standing helplessly holding the silent, weeping woman's hand, the nurse came to get me. Her hurried pace and strained face told me there was a problem with my husband. He was not well. I felt terrible leaving this woman, but I did. I had to.

The decision was made to admit my husband and he would need to be transferred out of radiation, over to the emergency room. As we were leaving the examination room, I stopped at the threshold, turned, and went back in. I grabbed the box of tissue from the receptionist's desk; I didn't know why.

At the emergency room, we were told to go into the waiting room until called. Unbelievably, in the middle of the room, another woman was there sitting alone, crying uncontrollably, using a sodden, mangled tissue over and over.

An immense heaviness settled on my shoulders. Their tears adding bricks to my overburdened, too heavy backpack. Too much pain. Too much solitude. Too much despair. Why couldn't I find the words to help these women? Find some way to take bricks out of their backpacks. Ease their burdens. I looked down, and saw a crushed tissue box in my hands and I understood why I had taken it.

I approached the weeping woman and handed her the box, patted her on the shoulder. She didn't speak, could only shake her head and everything in that moment was clear.

When we are standing in the lowest level of Hell, it is our nature to look up, seek help and guidance, deliverance and strength. But, maybe what we really need to do is look all around us. There are others who are here, in this lowest level, only they're not able to stand, not able to sit. They are lying curled in the fetal position at our feet. It is to them that we need to reach out, to help them stand up, brush off the dust, and pat them on the back.

I don't want to be on this journey through Hell, but since I am, I need to remember to stop and help those lying along the road get back up onto their feet.

We are stronger in this walk, when we walk together.

Day 20: One of the hardest parts about cancer is telling people. How do you tell hundreds of family and friends that someone you love has just been diagnosed with cancer?

We decided that, given the number of people we know, we would take a weekend to personally tell a few dozen people, and then we would use social media, so everyone would have the same information at the same time.

Most people reacted with about the same responses: "What can we do to help you?" "Prayers being sent out daily for you" "We hope your husband has a speedy recovery."

Then there was the reaction of one man, who I told face to face. His response was:

"Okay."

In works of fiction, sometimes characters in a rage describe seeing their world suddenly colored red in response to their inner rage. I can say definitively, no red colored my vision. Instead, a weird clarity of sight took hold of me.

Every line, pore, and hair on his face became crystal clear. I went from zero to one million on the anger scale with the utterance of this loathsome word, and I felt my fists clench. I envisioned my much feared right upper cut, slamming into his jaw. Instead of acting on these primal instincts, I took a deep breath, flared my nostrils and tried again.

"He'll have to undergo chemotherapy and radiation."

"Okay."

"His hair will fall out and he may be sick."

"Okay."

"We're going to need to build a dome over our home and pump in
purified air."

"Okay."

"We'll be growing organic fruits and veggies under the dome to reduce his pesticide exposure."

"Okay."

"We contacted the Alpha Centurians and in exchange for our three children that they will use as lab animals for experiments, we'll be getting the Inner Space Galactic Anti-Cancer Serum that they sell."

"Okay."

Okay, I got it. Here was someone who had made it through life without ever having found himself standing on that lower ring of Hell, floundering around for a life-saver.

Here was someone who hadn't waded through the sewer of life, smelling the fear, despair, desperation, and hopelessness that lives there. Here was someone who couldn't relate because pain, suffering and exhaustion hadn't colored his world.

I realized that, if given the choice to live the last almost five decades of my life how I had lived it, or switch with this person, I would never switch. Sure, there have been terrible lows, moments of dark despair, and periods where no light could be seen.

But when the darkness cleared, the joy, happiness, and celebration of life was so much richer for having been down there. Standing in that lower ring of Hell for periods of time, cleared my vision and let me see the world around me in a better light. I was stronger, more enriched and able to celebrate the good times with a greater passion and a deeper gratitude.

And maybe, this man was right in his assessment. We have a little cancer in our home right now, but it will be gone soon.

"Okay."

Day 21: We're having some short-term memory issues here. Chemo drugs? Chemo Fog? Exhaustion? Some insidious combination of the three? Not sure, but each day has become an adventure as we seek out misplaced shoes, wallets, car keys, jackets, children, animals, and important papers.

The sad thing is, it's not just my husband. Sure he has Chemo Fog, that weird mental dampening caused by the chemotherapy drugs. He finds himself in the middle of a sentence, unsure of what he was just saying or what point he was trying to make. Besides his train of thought, he loses personal items too. But I can't seem to keep track of things either, as if the Chemo Fog is oozing from my husband's pores, gathering over my head and smothering me too. This phantom fog of forgetfulness throughout our home is causing us to lose what is most important to us each day.

A few weeks ago, I lost our van at the hospital. I had left my husband outside the hospital after his chemotherapy was over, he being too weak to walk the three blocks to the parking garage. I made a mad dash to the parking lot knowing that each passing minute was a step closer to the start of the inevitable vomit that now seemed to piggyback onto each chemotherapy treatment.

I stopped a block away from the parking garage, convinced I had actually given the van to the valet that morning instead. I switched back, running toward the valet. A block away from the valet, I stopped again, realizing I had definitely parked the van in one of the three hospital parking lots, only I wasn't sure which one it was in.

All these switchbacks were performed in front of a police officer and a woman waiting to cross the street. I finally stopped in front of them, looked the officer straight in the face and said, "I seem to have lost my van. I've also lost my mind, and I'm hoping I left it in my van, so it's important that I find my van."

The woman snickered and I thought the officer would probably arrest me as I was clearly a menace to society. I could see the headlines across the city newspaper, "Cop Saves City From Sleep Depraved Lunatic," with a picture of me in my hot-pink 80's windbreaker and plaid beige pants, because that morning, they were the only two clothing items I could find that were clean. Instead, he looked me directly in the eye and said, "Check your pockets and wallet."

Huh?

He was right of course. The parking lot stub was in my pocket and he was able to direct me to my van. Luckily, when I got there, I found my mind was sitting in the back seat along with a pair of sunglasses, three jackets, one of which was actually made in this decade, the kitchen sink, some marbles, an old teddy bear, a vomit-encrusted pillow, a plate of ten-day-old nacho's, an unmarked bottle containing a mystery liquid that resembled a high school science project gone wrong, and some loose change.

With relief I got in and drove home, only to realize that I had forgotten my husband at the hospital....

Week 4: Where Am I?

Day 22: Half over isn't always the answer that we want to hear.

Like when you're traveling with small children from Chicago to Florida with a broken radio that only plays one cassette tape. When one of them asks, "Are we there yet?" and you have to answer, "We're just halfway there, which means another 12 hours of Veggie Tales Christmas Tunes." Half over is not the answer anyone in the van wants to hear at that moment.

Or when the nurse says, "How is that root canal going?" and the dentist replies, "I'm almost half over with removing it" and you already screwed your courage to the sticking point ten minutes ago, so there's nothing left.

But sometimes, half over is *amazing*. Today was a Half Over day. My husband is now halfway over with radiation!!!! As long as each day has seemed, and as long as each week has been, we are already at a milestone in this journey! Maybe the worst is behind us. Maybe my backpack will feel lighter tomorrow morning when I reach over to pick it up.

My husband still has a way to go in his recovery, but today we'll put up a small victory sign, as the little cancer that invaded our home is even smaller than it was three weeks ago.

Too bad today's house cleaning isn't half over, though.

Day 23: Flashback: *I stand on the threshold of this newly mounded grave and feel the world start to spin out of control. Overhead, thunder cracks hard against my skull and I feel the hair on my bare arms rise as the lightning strikes nearby. The skies open up and hard jagged sheets of rain slice my body to ribbons. Pieces of me fall onto the earth, falling, falling, so near this grave. Lying in a fetal position on the ground near the open maw of earth, I wonder if I'll join her.*

My husband hovers over me, shielding me from the tormenting rain. "Can you get up?" he asks, not realizing that I have no voice. "We need to be out of this rain. We have to leave," he pleads. I am dimensionless. Voiceless. Without substance or form. He picks me up and carries me to the truck.

He starts the engine and fires up the heater. As I smell my own dampness mixed with my misery, two lone words bubble up from some dark recess in my soul and burst forth.

"I can't," I say to him.

My husband of only a few years hears, and he knows. He knows what I mean.

I can't continue to work these sixty-hour weeks.

I can't continue the daily commute into the city for fertility treatments anymore.

I can't handle him working a different shift than me, so we only see each other on Sundays and at funerals.

I can't take the death that has surrounded us these past fourteen months, finding us at funerals eleven times.

I just plain can't.

My husband of just a few years, though, can. And he does. He bears the weight for the two of us, just long enough for me to get back on my feet again. Until I can, again.

Today: *It's been over twenty years since that crushing day at our dear great aunt's grave. Many mountains have been climbed, many valleys walked through. Today is Day 1 of Round 2 of chemotherapy, making it a day that we climb the mountain and feel like we're in the valley at the same time. Today is also a day when I carry the load as much as possible for my husband.*

I will.

I must.

I can.

Day 24: Lately, there are days that I find myself holding my breath at random times. It's as if I'm anticipating something that remains nameless, hiding just around the next corner for me, waiting to pounce when I least expect it. Something that is shapeless, outside of my grasp. A breath held tight within my chest in expectation of a phone call with bad news or a whispered moan indicating the pain level is spiking. A breath saved up for that moment when it will feel like the wind has been knocked out of me and that the floor has dropped out all at the same time.

These periods of restless anticipation seem to coincide with those days when I wake up feeling un-rested, weary from this journey. Those mornings, when reaching down for the proverbial backpack, the weight feels too ponderous and impossible to shoulder. I am only able to stand crouched under its load, struggling to draw breath, incapable of too many steps.

During those moments, a quiet voice in the back of my mind sends out sibilant prompts to me to keep moving forward. It reminds me to stand as tall as possible, with my head up. To make sure I do not fall under the ponderous weight of this over-filled backpack.

The voice whispers throughout the day, constantly reminding me.

Inhale.

Exhale.

Breathe.

Day 25: *5:06 a.m.* I woke up late and felt the panic surge through me. Not today, I couldn't be late today, the third day of chemotherapy, the worst one. It meant my husband went to bed vomiting last night, and woke up vomiting this morning. I swung my feet over the side of the bed, and the headache that had been a small blossom, sprang into full bloom. Unbelievably, I'm going through menopause again, round two, and today hormones long gone, opted for a group sit-in over my left eye. I went in search of coffee and some aspirin.

5:45 a.m. We are really late now. I was trying to decide how many vomit bags and towels it would take to get my husband out of the bathroom, down two flights of stairs and into the van. How many times can someone vomit when they haven't eaten in twelve hours? I had dumped three medications into him, yet the Rainbow Riot continued, great gushing geysers, no relief in sight. I waited for a break in the action, then rushed in with towels, bags, tissues. "Come on, we have to go," was all I could offer him. Where are the right words when you need them? Struggling to shoulder the backpack, it felt heavier than it had ever felt. I longed to dump it back onto the floor and climb back into bed and just call the whole day off.

6:11 a.m. We were finally getting onto the highway. We had been on our way earlier, but of course the van had a flat tire, so we had to turn around, and unload everything into the car. Besides consuming precious time, this also prompted the Rainbow Riot there in the driveway. How many flat tires on how many cars can one family have in one week? As this was the second one for us this week, I decided the answer had better be two. I really had reached my limit for flat tires. I wrestled internally with whether it would be a good idea if the neighbor's dog cleaned up the vomit in the driveway before I got home, or if this would be a bad thing to let happen. Had the menopause migraine not been raging above my left eye when the vomit occurred, I might have clearly thought to throw my pajama pants onto the heap of steaming unidentified goo. It was in the hands, or should I say paws, of the neighbor's dog now.

6:24 a.m. Snake crawling on the expressway, this became my new definition of madness. We lurched forward, gunning it to 30 m.p.h., only to slam on the brakes after only 37 seconds of driving. There were thousands of us, not hundreds, and I wondered about the sheer magnitude of all those people trying to get to work, home or wherever. Why call it an expressway, when there's nothing express about it? We certainly can't call it a freeway, as there's no freedom from the congestion and endless traffic. I was also angry that the menopause induced hormone tidal wave crashing through my system had made me oversleep. What kind of a world makes a woman go through menopause twice, and then, in an ironic twist, decides she should have to go through it while her husband is battling cancer?

6:33 a.m. Why is this happening? Why today? Why did I wake up late? Why did the van have a flat and making us go back? Why is traffic so horrendously worse than it has ever been? Why, why, why? I clench the steering wheel even tighter, gritting my teeth, causing the migraine to crescendo into a soaring, dipping, driving pain. Why? Why? Why? This one-word mantra taps in my brain, drowning out all other thoughts.

6:47 a.m. And there it was. The reason I woke up late. The reason my husband was so sick. The reason the van had a flat tire. The reason the traffic had delayed us. We had to be there, at that point on the highway, at precisely that moment. It was truly magnificent and it took my breath away. It made all the tension drain from me, filling me with nothing but wonderment and thankfulness.

Just past the second-to-last exit, just as the traffic finally broke free, the city loomed like a smoky-grey charcoal drawing, majestic, regal, quiet. But that was not what took my breath away. No. It was the sky beyond. Incredible slashes of buttery-yellow, gunmetal grey, peacock blue. No artist could emulate this. No photographer could capture this. The view of the sunrise, creeping over the eastern horizon was breath-taking, awe inspiring, peaceful.

That was what I was meant to see. The gift I was meant to be given this morning, when the backpack was laboriously heavy. That was what I was meant to experience this morning and why everything happened the way it did. That was what I'm now grateful for.

Anyone can love a sunset, because it allows the viewer to feel relief that another day is done. But it takes someone special to appreciate the beauty in a sunrise, for this sings out opportunity.

A new day to get it right. A new day to reach out and help those around us. A new day to celebrate. A new day to rejoice. If you missed the sunrise this morning, set the alarm to go off early tomorrow and get up in time to see the "show." It's worth the price of admission.

Day 26: Flashback, Oct. 1983: *Despite the sun overhead beating down bright and strong, we're huddled under a blanket as the air contains an edge of winter to it. With my best friends on either side of me, we giggle and shiver, waiting for kick off. Sitting on the cold, metal bleachers in the stadium, we feel the energy of everyone around us, and we're swept up in it. This is college football at its finest.*

The game commences, the crowd roars, the wind bites our faces, but suddenly I am blind to it all. It's as if I have tunnel vision and tunnel hearing, shutting down everything but the feeling in my right hand and arm. I do not see, I do not hear. All because my best friend, a boy from high school, has taken my hand under the blanket, causing an energy surge that has blasted through me. I'm convinced that everyone around me can see sparks and lights bursting from the pores on my face and head. It's inconceivable that such a small gesture can have such a profound effect on me, and yet, it has.

We've been friends for years, nothing more, just good friends. This one, simple, physical connection has changed everything. Everything is different now. The world seems more beautiful, the light brighter, sounds clearer. This is either the beginning of a great

relationship, or the end of a beautiful friendship. I squeeze
his hand and decide to let Fate take me where it will…

Today: My son and I were running late to pick up my husband from chemotherapy. This day of all days, we needed to be on time. The third session of chemotherapy weeks are always the worst, leaving my husband almost transparent, weakened, diminished. We pulled up to the hospital entrance and couldn't find him, his usual bench vacant in the waning sunlight. A frantic ten minutes went by as my son walked the corridors of the hospital, searching for his father. My husband and son finally converged on the car at the same time, coming from different ends of the hospital. I exhaled, not realizing how long I had been holding my breath.

We hit the expressway, punching into the grid lock by sheer force. I looked over to check on my husband, and realized somehow, he was even more translucent than moments ago, as if his physical presence was fading before my eyes.

I was gripping the steering wheel with two hands, desperate to steer the automobile ship through the traffic storm in front of us. But seeing my husband, I decided that he needed human contact more than the car needed guidance, so I reached for his hand.

It was cold, damp, unfamiliar, yet I knew this hand as well as my own. Here was the hand that rocked our babies, fixed washing machines, chopped down Christmas trees. Here was the hand that when it slipped into mine at a football game twenty-nine years ago, set us on the path that we continue on today. Despite the chaos that I was churning through with that hunk of metal, the connection with my husband was more important, and so we stayed like that for most of the ride.

The question that I asked myself later was, "Which of us really needed that connection more?"

Day 27: After my shower this morning, I reached for my towel on the rack and froze. My towel was there, on the front rack like usual, but my husband's towel, which normally hangs on the back rack, was missing. Seeing that lone towel hanging forlornly on the rack, sent ice water down my spine. Some chilling thoughts bloomed in my head, "What if he doesn't make it? What if I am alone some day?"

My days would start like this, confronted by just one towel hanging on a double towel rack meant for two. I would probably still make too much coffee, as we seem to always have three extra cups leftover each morning even now. The laundry would never get done, as my back prevents me from carrying the baskets up and down the three flights of stairs in our home. The computer would eventually get a virus and die a tragic death, for I am without skills in this area. The lawn would not get mowed, clocks would not get fixed, and snow would not be shoveled. Each night would find me, alone on the couch, afraid to touch the remote control, because it is not something I ever handle, as I am technologically impaired.

Who would I go to weddings with? Who would walk our daughter down the aisle someday at her wedding? Who would be my partner when playing cards and on the golf course? Who would I argue with, laugh with, despair with, rejoice with?

I did not start out in life as half of a pair, but somewhere between my birth and now, that is what I became. Sometime, long, long ago, I said good-bye to my single life, and hello to a life built around him, with him, next to him.

Cancer needs to leave our home and do it soon. I'm weary from this struggle, exhausted from the weight of the load that I carry each day. But mostly, I just need to know that my future will still include being a part of a pair, at least for a while longer, and not as a broken, battered small ship left adrift in a vast ocean alone and lost.

Week 5: I'll Always Leave the Light On For You

Day 29: Flashback: Feb 1994: I time my trip so I will be with my best girlfriend during the third week after her chemotherapy. These are her highest energy days, so we can get the most out of my visit.

We hit the Farmer's Market early to buy seafood for our dinner that night. An amazing indoor warehouse, the seafood hawkers literally throw your food to one another as they shout out your orders. It's a loud, crowded, collection of vendors from all over the world. I tell my friend I somehow feel at home here. She laughs, and for a moment we both forget that she has cancer.

Later, we meet our friends at a bar for fried green tomatoes and beers. I bite into one for the first time in my life and say, "Why the hell do you people eat these? They're terrible." My friend replies, "We don't know any better." We drink more beers, and for the rest of the evening, we forget that she has cancer.

Around 1 a.m., we leave the bar and head home. Having eaten and drunk our way through the city, I'm ready to just go to sleep. My friend though, behind the

wheel and in control of the car, screams, "HOT DAMN
THE LIGHT IS ON," cranks the steering wheel hard to the
right, hitting the curb as we turn into the parking lot. We
find ourselves at the drive through window of a fast food
restaurant I have never heard of before that specializes in
hot-out-of-the-fryer donuts. She's practically shouting as
she orders six doughnuts and two hot chocolates with extra
whipped cream.

"Have you lost your mind? I'm not eating anything,
I would puke if I did," I inform her. She laughs, hands me a
doughnut and despite my misgivings, I pop it into my
mouth. Somehow, I'm magically transported to some donut
filled Utopia on earth. We're not even out of the parking lot
and four doughnuts are gone. We laugh, snort, giggle and
choke, as we try to outdo each other describing these
incredible gifts from Heaven in the form of fried dough.
And for awhile, we forget that she has cancer.

We drive to a local park, deserted at this hour of the
morning, and park the car. It's chilly, but not unpleasant,
so we get out and stroll along, neither of us speaking. Time
is slipping away for us, both in this weekend and in life
itself, but we don't feel the need to fill the silence with
empty words. For now, it is enough to merely be in each
other's presence, in the present, forgetting about cancer.

My beautiful friend eventually lost her fight with cancer, but in that amazing weekend that we spent together, she reminded me, that this journey is short, no matter how much time we're given and if the light is on, whether it's at an all-night donut shop, a friend's house, or wherever you are standing, you should stop and take time to rejoice in that light, rest in that light, celebrate the light.

And if the choice is doughnuts or fried green tomatoes… well my friend, I know what I'm going for.

Day 30: When my husband's hair fell out, it was almost overnight. One day a few strands on the pillow, the next day huge clumps that clogged the shower and sink. It was easier to simply shave his head and be done with the hair for awhile.

Drastic in the change, it took me a few days to get used to seeing him without hair. Eventually though, I managed.

The thinning of the skin, the color slowly changing from a healthy, rosy glow to an unearthly, unnatural sallow is never something I adjust to when being around cancer patients though. They universally look like they have gone to a brink of existence that they cannot possibly come back from. Surely no one that looks that gravely ill, could possibly recover and have their skin return to a normal color.

They do though. Time and time again, as I've sat with family and friends who have battled cancer, I have seen them walk up to the precipice of death, spit in its eye and then turn around and walk back toward good health. It can be done.

It's just hard to imagine my husband making that return. When looking at his papery, translucent skin, the angry eruptions from boils on the back of his head and the lack of hair over his entire body, recovery is hard to imagine.

This is the man who has always been physically active and is now reduced to napping multiple times per day, just to make it to dinner time. This is the man who could play full court basketball for two hours and still come home to mow the lawn on Saturdays, but now cannot even help load the dishwasher at night. This is the man who always looked healthy and happy in all the pictures that I torture myself with, late at night, when I can't sleep searching for the point in our lives where we made a mistake and allowed this angry monster, cancer, to enter our home.

I know my husband will recover and life will go on. It has to, because I cannot see any other future than that one right now.

Day 31: Today is my husband's birthday. On any given year, birthday presents are difficult to find, as we've hit that point in our lives where we have everything we want and need.

For my son though, he popped awake early this morning, came into the kitchen and told me what he wanted to give his dad as a birthday gift. It was a simple request, yet so eloquent, it made my heart swell and ache, all at once. It made me realize, that no matter what we have in terms of money, resources and material possessions, it's still those beautiful gestures of the heart that remain the most amazing gifts we can give to one another.

The gift was simple. He asked me to buzz off all of his hair. He wanted to look like dad.

So, as the sun rose behind me, I cut off all of my son's hair.

The rest of my husband's gift was equally simple.

Happy Birthday; I gave you our children, I gave you 24 years of marriage, I gave you through sickness and health, I gave you through poverty and still to come wealth, I gave you my best, and sadly, my worst, I gave you my all.

Happy Birthday; I give you another 24 years of marriage, I give you 24 more years of through sickness and health (let's emphasize health here), I give you 24 more years of minimal poverty and hopefully that elusive wealth, I give you 24 more years of my best and let's be done with the worst, I give you 24 more years of my all.

Let's make them grand.

Day 32: Cancer doesn't discriminate.

It's the great equal opportunist. All races, all ages, both genders, its "Welcome Sign" is always on, its door is always open.

We don't willingly walk through this door, we just find ourselves somehow in the building, sitting at the desk, filling out the application.

I see this when I sit in the radiation waiting room. I sometimes assign names and personas to the "dailies" that are there, to help pass the time.

There's Miss USA 1967. Regal, stick-thin, her makeup and clothes, while old and faded, are clean and well put together. Every time I speak with her, I ponder what would happen if she found herself in my closet. I'm convinced it would cause her more pain and discomfort than the radiation and chemotherapy. I also wonder if there is a Hot Mess USA competition. I know that's one competition I would win hands down.

There's the Asian Wonder Twins. Not sure actually if they're siblings or an old married couple. Exactly the same height, build, features, they complement each other like a beautiful song. They move around the waiting room as one, fussing over each other in their native tongue. The adjective of Wonder is added to describe them because neither of them appear to be sick, and as both always go back into the treatment area, I'm always left wondering which one has cancer.

There's Mabel and Mavis, two African-American sisters who fight, bicker, argue, cuss and annoy each other and everyone around them. Their conversation amuses, entertains, bothers and exhausts us, as we focus on them and not the constant kindergarten-level political analysis spewing from MSNBC or FOX news on the flat screen. New onlookers may be convinced that Mabel and Mavis have scratched, slapped and kicked their way through the fifty plus years they've been siblings, until the one sister is called back for treatment and the transformation occurs. These two have each others' backs and their love for one another is truly limitless. It is at its simplest, what is meant by the word 'sister.'

Then there's John Wayne Steroid. Larger than life, he fills up part of the waiting room with his physical presence, then sucks the remaining air from the rest of the room with his daily complaint about the coffee only being available for patients. He patrols the small room like a shark, looking for small, unsuspecting minnows that he can swoop down on, sit next to, and eat up with his droning litany about how the coffee should be available for everyone. I tolerate him for a few days, but on one of my down days, I let him have it, informing him and everyone there, that I will personally buy him a coffee from across the street, just let me know how he takes it. This brings all conversation to a halt, as we wait to see if the purple red of John Wayne Steroids face will result in a stroke. He gets up and walks out, and life goes on.

We don't have to *enjoy* our time in cancer's employ, we just have to *do* our time, get through each day, looking forward to the "vacation" time when we move on from this "job."

Before we leave though, maybe we could look in on the employee lounge at Cancer Inc. and learn a thing or two about diversity, equality, tenacity, courage and compassion.

Day 33: It's been over a month now and I thought, incorrectly it seems, that the backpack would somehow be getting lighter with each passing day. I honestly thought that each treatment would represent a brick being removed from the backpack, giving my daily steps more bounce and energy as time went on.

That hasn't been the case. If anything, each morning it becomes harder and harder to get out of bed and face the day. I wake, sometimes in the middle of the night and spend the rest of the hours, not trying to fall back asleep, but to psyche myself up for the upcoming day. Trying to motivate myself to just survive whatever chaos is thrown in my face and do so, with a smile on my face so others don't see how desperately sad I am inside.

True, it's helped that friends and family have been dropping off meals and helping with carpools whenever they can. This has eased the burden somewhat. It's just that, there always seems to be unseen, random upheavals that arise each day, in the form of broken dishwashers, missing wallets, clogged toilets, and oceans of unexpected vomit, that derail my good intentions of seeking out a normal day.

It also doesn't help that now we know what to expect. Knowing that the vomit will hit a crescendo on days three and four of the chemotherapy weeks, somehow the anticipation makes it that much worse when it happens. Knowing that the heparin flush will result in a nasty, salty taste at the back of my husband's throat makes his anxiety peak just before the flush occurs. Knowing that the tumor is still in my husband's leg, waiting for the time when the chemotherapy has finally made it safe enough to remove it, makes the worry about it spreading seem all consuming. None of this was part of our old, normal, routine, only indications of our "new normal."

If I'm honest, maybe that is at the heart of what I am feeling. I miss the old normal. I miss those days where I didn't have to battle rush hour traffic both ways in the morning to get my husband into the city for treatment. Racing home in time to wake the boys and get them to school on time. Frantically, reversing the schedule in the afternoon, when I fight my way back through traffic into the city to pick up my diminished, wane husband from the chemotherapy room.

I miss Friday afternoons spent with friends and a good bottle of wine, leisurely slipping into the weekend. I miss dinners spent around our kitchen table, hearing about misadventures the boys had at school that day. I miss weekday trips up north to visit my daughter at college. I miss Sundays spent watching football games, eating too many appetizers and hurling insults at the teams on the television, as if they can hear us and we can affect the outcome of the games.

The backpack feels ponderously heavy, slowing my mental tread more and more each day. I want my old life back.

Day 34: So, we all know that time is relative. We've experienced it throughout our lives.

When you make the mistake of letting Blind Date From Hell pick you up, instead of meeting him at the restaurant, the three hours that he talks (and weeps) about his ex-girlfriend feel more like three life times. "You had a great time and want to call me again? Really? Well, I charge $190 per hour for therapist fees. Call my office manager and she'll set up our next 'date'...."

There's the slowing of time when your two-year-old son throws a fit at the library, peeling his clothes off, shrieking. You're trying to grab him, your four-year-old, your newborn baby, his clothes, the diaper bag, and your purse, all under the horrified eyes of those who are obeying the Please Be Quiet Universal Implied Code of Libraries. No matter how many steps you take toward the exit, it seems like time has slowed to a standstill and you will never get there. Of course, time slows even more, when you do make the exit and realize there's a blizzard outside and you are carrying a naked two-year-old.

Then there's Cancer Time which both slows and accelerates due to Chemo Fog, everyone's buddy PAIN, and Vomitus All-the-Time-ous. Cancer Time dips, soars, jumps, gaps, and moves like an old wooden roller coaster that has been in a constant state of disrepair for decades. You're never sure what is around the next corner and you don't really want to know, but you can't slow down the ride and get off, so you just hang on.

Cancer Time slows down, when you need it to speed up. Sit in the chemotherapy ward, watching the toxic chemicals drip into my sleeping husbands arm, I beg Cancer Time to speed up, asking that the six hours be condensed down into two. Somehow, though, the six hours feel like eight, or eighteen, or eighty hours, depending on how many patients are moaning in pain or discomfort, as the IV's drip their caustic solutions and time drags to a stand-still.

Then there are those times, when Cancer Time does speed up, practically flying by, like elusive grains of sand in the palm of your hand. You do everything in your power to protect and keep every precious minute, but the harder you try, the faster the grains of sand escape your cupped palms. These are the moments, when you are running late, due to exhaustion, vomiting, cramping, pain, or flat tires. When you desperately need just an extra five or ten minutes, to set everything in order, or to just find some order, in the chaos that you are surviving. This is when

Cancer Time speeds up to a break neck pace, time whizzing by you, escaping you like your shadow in a darkened room.

Yesterday, I actually lost an entire week due to Chemo Fog and Chemo Time, and I'm not even the cancer patient. That's not good. I'm supposed to be regulating time for us. I'm supposed to be tracking time for us. I'm not supposed to be affected by Chemo Fog. Yet, somehow, I was.

So, as of right now, my husband has SIX more radiation treatments. Which, given that time is relative, is less than the twenty-two he needed weeks ago, but more than the two that I thought he had left yesterday.

The one thing I do know for sure is that, it is Friday, and even though it's 11:04 a.m. here, it's 5:04 p.m. in Dublin right now, so as far as I'm concerned, Cancer Time is now on hold and the weekend has started.

I do hope someone calls me on Tuesday and makes sure I know that the weekend is over though… who knows what fog I'm going to be walking around in this weekend.

Day 35: It's quiet here. My husband is still asleep, kids are asleep and the cats haven't come into the office to shred paper yet. This is all important.

It's important, because when you have cancer, sleep becomes an elusive, slippery, oily fish, that wriggles and flips through your fingers. Oh, you may be able to catch and hold the fish for a short time each night, but it will escape you, swimming far away for hours and hours.

Eventually, the cancer patient starts spending part of their day obsessing about this rare fish, devising new ways to hook it and keep it. They look for it everywhere they are, hoping that this is the moment that they are able to grab hold and hang on for a few hours. The fish is, after all, beautiful, peaceful, calming, but only if the cancer patient can catch it and hang on to it.

Sometimes, it's just a matter of bait. What to use to catch that sneaky fish? A lump of OTC's? A mound of melatonin? A cocktail of prescriptions? All of them together? Each night the cancer patient trudges wearily down to the river Lethe and casts a line in, trying the bait of choice that night. Will the fish bite? Will it hold on, long enough to make it through the night? The patient stands on the riverbank full of hope and desire, willing the fish to bite hard.

I don't know if last night's bait was what caught the fish for my husband, or if it was simply that he stayed up late to enjoy the company of our daughter who was home for the weekend. Perhaps it was both. I do know that he's still asleep, and for this avid fisherman, I hope his dreams are filled with muskies and bass, and that he wakes restored and rested.

Week 6: There Are Worse Things in Life Than Cancer

Day 36: Last night was my cousin's daughter's wedding. The bride was beautiful, the groom was sweet, and it was so much fun to dance and act silly with family again.

But the whole day was colored with an eerie grey wash because of cancer.

It started with me forgetting that time runs differently when cancer has warped the clock. My husband was asleep when he was supposed to be getting ready. People were stopping by with food when I was supposed to be getting ready. When I did finally go to get ready, I grabbed the purple spray can from the bathroom closet, meaning to use some hairspray in some feeble attempt at fashion and at the last minute, my brain registered that the spray can said, "Bathroom Blaster!" on it. An aerosol spray can of hard core chemical cleaners for the shower, who knows how many hours would have been spent in the local ER had I not caught myself at the last minute. This wouldn't have been the first time some fashion disaster had occurred moments before leaving the house, but for some reason, with cancer coloring the day grey, I was left a bit tremulous and shaky from the near miss.

It also colored the wedding reception a watery, misty, ashy grey, when my husband had to leave after dinner to go home to sleep. That he had made it through the wedding and dinner was an achievement in itself. That he had shown up to the reception wearing a hippie-style Halloween costume wig to hide his bald head, was an even greater achievement for it showed a sliver of the man he was before cancer. The one who loved joking and kidding around with my family at past family gatherings before cancer took away most of our humor. The one who would never take life too seriously before cancer invaded our home.

Had he been able to stay, he would have taken up a post at the guy's table, where they had a grand view of the dance floor, but from which they refused to budge. Leaving us women to shake, boogie and lurch around the floor in a throwback to our early youth, when our movements were still fluid. Why it mattered to me that he was not sitting there, I'm not entirely sure, but it did.

The evening ended after midnight and it should have seen my husband and I driving home in that comfortable silence that comes after a quarter of a century together. Instead, it was a pleasant enough drive with my daughter as designated driver, chatting about the silly things, the beautiful things, the clever things that the day had held. But as the exhaustion set deep into my bones during the drive home, the grey wash deepened to a darker shade, coloring my recollections of the day with that one thought, it had been a day apart. I had been alone, even though I was in a room full of people.

There will be other weddings, births, reunions, and parties, where the grey wash is lifted. Other opportunities, when our vision has cleared of all sickness and cancer. Times when that beautiful silence will fill the car ride home with a level of communication that is only for two people who have lived most of their lives together. Until then, I'll just have to turn up the radio and sing in an off-key, loud voice and fill up that silence with my own grey wash.

Day 37: Flashback, March 16, 1945, 9:28 PM: She is only nine years old. She should be in bed. She should be sleeping, with Greta her favorite dolly that Oma gave her a long time ago, lying next to her.

Instead, she is here, crouched in the darkness of the cellar, shaking, sobbing, clinging to her mother, brother and father.

BOOM!

The Giant has woken, and taken his first steps. The heavy metallic thud of his enormous boots ringing through the night like an explosion, ripping through the sleepy silence of the town, ensuring that no one will sleep tonight. The floor shakes under their feet. The Giant's steps grow steadier, louder, nearer.

BOOM! BOOM!

"Mutti! Was ist los?" the girl wails (Mommy, what is happening?) as she finally finds her small, shaky voice.

"Ruhig Leibchen!" the mother scolds, (quiet my love) spitting the words out in a fierce whisper. The child realizes her mother is trying to quiet her so the Giant won't find them. Her terror steals her voice away.

BOOM! BOOM!

Her mother's grip on the girl and boy tightens, and she starts to sway slightly. Her voice, barely above a whisper, can be heard now, over and over, "Weiss ich sicher, Gott ist hier" (I always know, God is here) and the girl, recognizing this as the last line in a favorite prayer, joins in.

BOOM! BOOM!

Despite their being quiet, despite their prayers to God, the Giant approaches, gaining speed, his steps growing louder. The house shakes, windows rattle.

The father's voice rises above the din. "Unser Vater, der du bist im Himmel, geheiligt durch deinen Namen", the Lord's Prayer rains down on his wife, his son, his daughter. His agony, his fear, his helplessness pouring through the words, but his desperation to save his family from the Giant drives him to repeat the Lord's Prayer over and over. Louder and louder his voice. Louder and louder the Giant's steps. The house shudders, shakes, trembles.

BOOM! BOOM!

The Giant draws nearer.

Today: My children burst into my mother's home, transforming the quiet, restful atmosphere instantly into a cacophony of giggles, shrieks, and screams. At one, two and four years of age, their combined energy could power half the Midwest, and the energy of my mother's love for them, could cover the rest of the nation.

"Mutti! Was ist los?" I yell out, trying to locate my mom.

She's in the kitchen, the expression on her face a strange mask, one that I've never seen in the thirty-five years I've been alive.

"The cancer has spread to my brain," she says matter-of-factly.

My world shrinks. Contracts. Dims. I struggle to breathe. My children squeal as they chase the dog around, but I no longer hear them.

My entire being is emptied, then immediately filled with a white-hot rage.

"This totally sucks. I'm sick of this cancer. It's not fair. You don't deserve this. It's the worst thing and it shouldn't be happening to you."

"It's not the worst thing," she calmly replies.

"Are you out of your mind? What are you talking about?" I spit out.

"Sit down," she says quietly, "and I'll tell you about the night our town got bombed and almost everyone died. There are definitely worse things in this world than a little cancer."

Cancer eventually took my mother's life, but it never took her dignity from her, it never took her courage from her, and it never took her perspective from her. For her, it wasn't the worst thing. It was just another bump in the road of life, one that needed to be walked through and over. It was a private battle, waged within her body, and for her there was an acceptance, done with grace, that this battle at least would not leave thousands of people destroyed in its wake. By shouldering this fight by herself, she truly believed that others were spared.

Day 38: When dealing with cancer, no matter how you plan your day, life can change in a moment, and the best we can do is roll with it. Yesterday was one of those days.

My husband had complained of a few minor symptoms in the morning so he called his doctor. She told him to report to the lab for some tests after he was done with his radiation treatment. By 1:15 p.m. we were at home and had gone back to the daily routine.

At 3:34 p.m. the doctor called with the blood work results. Truly the definition of STAT when they're turning blood work over in a few hours. After a few minutes chatting with her, my husband got off the phone, and told me what they had said. Life changed in that instant. At that point, we are thrust into the NEUTROPENIA ZONE.

A secondary problem that some cancer patients experience, neutropenia is a depletion of the white blood cells. His immune system was functioning at a near zero level, the few white blood cells in his body having lost their way, and the world had become his worst enemy.

I whipped on the Wonder Woman Cleaning Cape, armed myself with rubber gloves, a bottle of 91% Alcohol, sterile wipes, paper towels, and went to battle with the surfaces in my home.

Is that the Evil *E.coli* lurking under the cabinet handles in the kitchen? Is there Creepy *Cryptosporidium* lunching in the bathroom tiles? Could there be *Staphylococcus* throwing a party in the lunch meat I bought a few days ago? I marched through my home, dowsing everything with alcohol, muttering Under, Under, Under quietly to remind myself to wipe under everything too.

My husband will get through this, most likely in just a few days, because he is, after all, young and fairly healthy. We'll go back to living in a germ-filled home, having germ coated visitors drop by and we'll take trips to germ-filled grocery stores.

Until then, I'll be wiping down surfaces with rubbing alcohol, and just to be on the safe side, I'm thinking it's my duty to drink a bottle of wine tonight, to kill any germs lurking inside of me. Gotta do my part and take one for the team.

Day 39: My cousin sent me an email today and the message was short, but profound. It said:

"What can be done with money without health?"

Whole lotta nothing, really. But somehow, somewhere along the journey, we forget this. We become so wrapped up in the pursuit of wealth that we shove health down on the list of priorities below money, fame and fortune. We focus not on taking care of ourselves, but amassing sums of money so we can purchase material possessions that we think will make us happier.

What if each day, our priority was focused on tasks that were beneficial to our health, instead of pursuing an ever higher salary or a bigger home? What if we valued an hour walk with the dog and children more than an hour spent earning money? What if we valued an hour spent meditating more than an hour spent shopping for trinkets for our home. What if we valued an hour participating in a sport or exercise more than an hour worrying about how to pay for our over-priced home?

I'm going to try to stop myself each time I say, "I need this" and repeat the statement as "I want this" instead. Then I'll take a moment to analyze whether it's really going to make me happy or not. "I need this sweater" implies that I am freezing to death and need a layer of clothing as protection from the cold, when in truth, I own a closet of sweaters, so I merely want another sweater. "I need a bigger home" implies that I'm living in a 200 square foot Tiny Home, along with my three kids, husband, dog, and two cats and we have managed to outgrow the space. When in reality, we just need to clean out a few closets and we would fit just fine in the modestly-sized home that we own. We don't need a bigger home, we just need less stuff.

Of course, certain things, like cookies, chocolate, and wine, will always remain on the "I need this" list having moved from the "I want this" list in my past when my addictions for these items got the better of me.

After all, what can be done with life without cookies, chocolate and wine?

Day 40: It's 4:00 p.m. here. Dinner should occur in about two hours. So, why are we having cookies and ice cream right now?

Because life is short.

Because life is really, really short.

Because life is really, really short and when faced with something like cancer, your perspective changes.

Because life is really, really short and when faced with something like cancer, your perspective changes and just getting through some days is hard enough, so cookies and ice cream before dinner makes it seem better.

Because we're given choices each day, and raised to make practical, wise decisions. We usually do, but sometimes, you just have to step outside of the norm, because in the end, life is really, really short.

In two hours I'll pull the Mystery Casserole out of the oven. Don't worry all you wonderful friends who have brought over food; it isn't from any of you. This pan of over cooked noodles, unnamed vegetables and unknown meat was generated by me about six months ago and with no label, it's anyone's guess what it contains. We'll all stare at it. We may pick at it. Even eat a little of it.

But tonight, when we go to bed, we won't go to bed hungry, because we made the practical, wise decision today to have cookies and ice cream for dinner, and Mystery Casserole for dessert.

I bet we have sweet dreams too.

Day 41: It started at 4 a.m. when I woke and found one of our cats sleeping on my left hip bone. As I was born breech, (how else would I enter this world than a$$ first?!?), the doctor used forceps, damaging my hip a bit. It's been a problem my whole life, but I've dealt with it. You wouldn't think a 10-pound kitty sleeping on my hip socket would matter, but matter it did. When my feet hit the floor, pain rocketed up and down the left side of my body. Ugh.

I grabbed a few Advil in the kitchen, then contemplated waiting to take the dog outside until they had kicked in. Our dog isn't exactly the patient kind, so waiting 30 minutes for a minor pain killer to take the edge off this pain was out of the question. I hobbled to the door, the dog almost knocking me over in her haste to get outside. I was half-way through the door when I realized I had forgotten to grab a jacket.

It was cold, crisp, and dark. I thought about going back in for a coat, but the number of steps it would take seemed like too many with my hip protesting. So I stood there and looked up into the sky. Good thing the hip was throbbing and I didn't go back for the jacket, because as I stood there, a star fell.

I thought, "Oh, now I get to make a wish!" And I did.

As I made my wish, I was reminded of one of my most cherished books, "The Gift of Acabar" by Og Mandino that my best friend gave me more than thirty years ago. This book was given to me when I had stepped off the path of grace. She helped me to regain my footing back then through the gift of this beautiful book.

It's about a star that falls to the ground, and a little boy who tries to fly it back up. The star gives him a beautiful gift called the Credenda, which are words to live by. The last few lines are these:

"Seek out those in need. Learn that he who delivers with one hand will always gather with two. Be of good cheer. Above all, remember that very little is needed to make a happy life. Look up. Reach out. Cling simply to God and journey quietly on your pathway to forever with charity and a smile. When you depart it will be said by all that your legacy was a better world than the one you found."

I don't know if my wish will come true. Maybe it's a little silly to even wish upon falling stars at my age. I hope it does come true though. It would be nice to be able to pick up that backpack one morning and find it filled with feathers and flowers for a change.

Day 42: My husband only has two radiation treatments left. Seriously, for real. I haven't miscounted or misplaced an entire week of my life this time. On Monday, he will leave the treatment center with his body cast and a bag of Ensure. This is the staff's idea of a graduation present.

But I suspect there are those who have had cancer who will understand when I say that these two remaining days of radiation are actually bittersweet. I suspect my husband will leave with his presents on Monday with a little heaviness in his heart.

No, he doesn't wish his cancer back so he could go through this again.

No, he won't be missing the actual treatment, which has left his leg, burned and sore.

What he will be missing is the radiation staff. His group of medical professionals who have left us in awe of their intelligence and education throughout his entire treatment cycle. Their caring, kind approach is what has set them well above most doctors we have encountered in our lives. I would like to think that I can describe these doctors in written words, but I can't. These are men and women who truly LISTEN. They are people who truly CARE. They are human beings who somehow, with their behavior, have redefined what a doctor should be, what a doctor could be.

We've been asked numerous times why we're commuting into the city each day for treatment, instead of staying out here in the 'burbs. This is why.

We wanted someone who would listen.

We wanted someone who would care.

We wanted someone who would save my husband's life.

Week 7: Isn't Today Wednesday?

Day 43: Flashback, April 8, 1999, 6:52 PM: The door whisks open with a strange sound of dry leaves on a grave site. Exhaustion, sadness, desperation, a whirlwind of emotions have tainted my perceptions, and now I'm convinced the Angel of Death is pushing the door open. My body tenses, my breath catches in my lungs, trapped there as the door continues to swing wide. In the dimly lit room, fear surges through me, for despite having sat here for fourteen days, waiting for this Angel, somewhere deep inside me, a voice screams, "NO! Please not yet!"

But it's not the Angel of Death, silently entering this room where the weary, comatose patient waits, but it is Angels, a whole flock of them, come to lift my burden, ease my aching heart, heal my tortured soul.

"We're sorry to disturb you. It's just that, we were talking, and your mother doesn't have long now. We wanted to say goodbye to her. We wanted to tell you both how much she means to us," says Anna Kay, mom's favorite nurse, approaching the bed where my mother lies. These Angels of Mercy, known to us as the day shift nurses gather

at my mom's bedside, each taking turns, pouring out their hearts at having known my mother during her two year long battle with cancer.

They turn to leave, and Anna Kay, sensing my desperation, comes back and places a gentle hand upon my shoulder. "Do not be afraid. Your mother has been waiting for something. We're not sure what it is, but she's close now, she will not make it to the dawn. You and your brother just need to be strong for a little bit longer." And then they're gone.

__8:34 p.m.:__ My brother, seated on my mom's right side, is holding her right hand in his left one. I, on the other side, am holding her left hand in my right, and across her broken, twisted body, we have joined our hands, creating a triangle of strength, a circle of love and hope unbroken. Still, I feel myself slipping into some dark place, falling, falling. In desperation, I look at my brother and say, "Remember when you sprayed that Coke all over the kitchen ceiling and none of us would confess to mom? We told her it was a fungus or mildew growing up there because she hadn't cleaned the ceiling in a long time. How we let her clean that ceiling thinking she had somehow missed mold growth for the entire summer? She was so pissed at all of us when we finally told her the truth." We laugh at the memory, the sound of our laughter drowning out the noise of my mother's labored breathing for a moment.

This memory and death bed confession lead us to more stories, and the night drags on, our laughter growing with intensity, as our voices start to fail. Still, we fill the passing minutes with all that our lives have been, and all that our mother has meant to us.

April 9, 1999, 3:58 a.m.: The door opens this time, not with a soft whisper, but with a larger than life whooshing noise, and Nurse Indignation storms in, barreling down on my brother and me like a tornado through the Midwest.

"QUIET!!! Your mother is trying to REST!!!" she spits out, in an authoritative whisper that she has practiced for years. This is meant to strike fear in our hearts, meant to put us in our place. Just loud enough to indicate the anger level it is being delivered with, but quiet enough to not wake sleeping patients. That my mother has been in a coma for two weeks and NOTHING is going to be waking her up, seems to not have registered with her. This isn't lost on me though, partly due to my absolute bone-deep exhaustion and partly from a strange sense of protection I *am feeling toward my unconscious mother from this seemingly threatening woman.*

My brother and I, survivors of life, beaten down, trodden upon, we have made it this far by holding onto one another, but more importantly, by hanging onto our humor, as an essential life saver. To be told to quiet the humor life-line that we are currently hanging onto doesn't sit well with either of us. We look at her and burst into loud, raucous laughter.

"OH, that is the BOMB! Our mother needs to REST?!? Who knew that being in a coma for two weeks was so taxing?!?!" I shriek, my exhaustion and sadness getting the better of me.

It's rude and insulting, but I can't help it. For fourteen days, my brother and I have taken turns sitting here, watching the life drain from our mother, breath by breath. We have not left her alone, not for one single minute during these last few weeks of her life and as we have watched her slip away, breath by breath, small parts of us have died along with her. Each time her breathing has stopped, one of us has stiffened up and fervently said, "NO," and then, miraculously, she has taken another breath. It has become our job to hold onto what little is left of her.

But now, the end is near, so the only gift left for us to give to her, is our humor, our stories, our memories, to let her know we are all right and that she did the best job she could raising us.

Nurse Indignation storms out, flames licking at her heels.

6:47 a.m.: *Unbelievably, my mother is still with us. I beg my brother to go with me to my home, for it's my daughter's seventh birthday. We'll grab showers, waffles and be there when she wakes up, take her to school, and be back here before too long. Mom will be fine, she's made it this far. He agrees to go and we leave our mother for the first time in fifteen days.*

8:01 a.m.: *We are back at the hospital, freshly showered, with lingering thoughts of sweet maple syrup in our minds. As we round the corner coming off the elevator, the sight of Anna Kay near the nursing station floods my system with ice water. She slowly walks toward us, keeping us from room 3305. "We finally realized what your mom has been waiting for these past fifteen days," Anna Kay gently says to us.*

I search her face for the answer, for this has been the mystery of the staff for the past two weeks. Despite all medical indications to the contrary, my mother has lasted long after the doctors have said she would pass away.

"What was she waiting for?" I croak, my voice spent from the stories told all night.

"She wanted to give your brother and you one final, beautiful gift, one that only a mother would know you want, that only a mother would know you need."

She pauses. I still don't know, my brother equally puzzled standing next to me.

"She wanted to spare you the moment that her Soul left this world. She was waiting for that one moment when both of you would be out of the room. This morning was the first time in fifteen days that it happened."

We tried to give the most beautiful gift to our mother, the gift of knowing that she had made a difference in our lives, that she had left an indelible mark on us and those around her, that she had loved and been loved. But in the end, she trumped us with her gift, that one gift that cannot be topped.

She gave us the gift of a Mother's Love.

Day 44: My husband's radiation treatments are completed. This should be a cause for celebration. It should feel like we climbed to the top of Mt. Everest and we're throwing a huge oxygen-deprived party up there, celebrating our achievement and the amazing feeling of conquering the climb.

But we're not, because he still has four rounds of chemotherapy and surgery to get through. So, we've climbed the mountain, we're oxygen-starved at the top, but all we can think about is the climb back down. The path is no less rocky on the back side of the mountain. There are still obstacles in our way and we're still going to need our loving, supportive sherpas (aka: family and friends) to help guide us down that unknown path.

It was difficult for him to leave for chemotherapy this morning. I've noticed this before as a caretaker. Rounds 3 and 4 are the most difficult. It's that point in the journey where you are at the crest of the mountain, you look around, and because you are so far into the trip, you cannot find the familiar. You cannot see the end. You are so weary from the trip already taken, that you don't think you can muster the energy to go on. But you do.

This Friday, he will officially be half way through with treatment. My husband will celebrate by having an

extra bag of IV fluids and sleeping most of the weekend.
On Monday, he'll start the journey down the back side of
the mountain, traveling that well-worn path toward
Recovery. You know the town, nestled at the base of Mt.
Cancer. Recovery is the stop over town, right next to our
final destination in that amazing city called Remission.

Day 45: The alarm fired off at 5:52 a.m., the precise time we should have been in our car, accelerating down the on-ramp, onto the expressway.

Uh, oh.

I screamed to my husband to move as I grabbed articles of clothing off the floor, assembling an outfit worthy of a front rack at a resale shop. I barked orders for him to get dressed, we had to GO, as I ran downstairs to make a quick cup of coffee.

I did a quick calculation to see how badly we were now behind. Thinking that I could regain time by channeling the long-gone spirit of Speed Racer, I gulped watery coffee and threw food into a bag for my husband's lunch. The shower fired off overhead. Are you kidding me? He's showering? With traffic times measured in Dog Years, every minute later we leave, seems to add seven minutes to the commute, and now he's decided to shower? ARG.....

I went outside and started up the car, let out the dog and cats, and caught my breath. I thought about Speed Racer and figured if I totally just shed all worries about traffic cops and drove like Speed Racer, then I would be able to make up some of the lost time. I went back into the house to find Speed Racer's trusty side kick, Chim-Chim.

He was in the kitchen, holding a crumpled envelope over the steam escaping from the broken coffee maker.

"Ummm, whatcha doin?" I asked, though the answer was pretty obvious.

"Steaming open this envelope," he replied without looking up.

"Right. Well, we're an hour late, so that's going to need to wait" (Meaning, put the envelope down, step away from the coffee maker, and no one will get hurt). He laid the envelope on top of the coffee maker, where seven hours later I found it permanently glued there.

The commute into the city was as it always is: congested, maniacal, colored by some form of weirdness. This week it was a ladder lying in the middle of the road (last week it was a live dog running around the highway). Coming down the off ramp, I'm pretty certain we were up on only two wheels taking the turn into the hospital drop off zone. With only three minutes to spare, I realized that somehow we had made the hour long drive in just under 35 minutes. Which meant, I must have been driving like some 5-hour energy drink, amped-up, Indy car driver. That I didn't get pulled over was either due to dumb luck or the fact that emergency personnel found the abandoned ladder more of a threat on the highway. You never know when those pesky ladders are gonna throw it into reverse and haul it out onto the middle lane, I guess.

I'm back now and the dust has settled. The rest of the day should be quieter. I still need to clean up the CSI blood training sites that one of our cats left all over our house when she sliced open her paw the other day. Paperwork long ignored needs to be filed, paid, or shredded by the cats. Laundry piled as high as Mount Everest in the utility room needs tackling. But, I've decided to leave the sodden, sticky envelope stuck to the top of the coffee maker. It's the yearly bill for the newspaper renewal and I'm left pondering why my husband would feel it necessary to steam this open when we were so grotesquely late already. It will be a quiet reminder each morning, that humor is the best way to start each day and patience is its own form of medicine.

Day 46: Chemo Fog is hard to define, but it happens sometimes during chemotherapy. For some, it's a mild, temporary dementia that distorts time and space. For others, short term memory is affected. Sometimes, both may occur or other odd symptoms arise.

Today, Chemo Fog was thick in the air in our home.

My husband came down into the kitchen and said, "Tomorrow you need to remember to pack my shot."

"I packed the shot with the water bottles. Today is Thursday."

"Isn't today Wednesday? Are you sure?"

"Positive. It's Thursday."

"If today is Thursday, then did you remember to pack the shot?"

"Yes, I packed the shot with the water bottles."

We got into the car amid blankets, pillows, tissues, mints, water bottles, barf bags, crackers, and trash. As I am backing out of the driveway, I feel the back end of the car rise up on my side, clearly indicating that I have run over something. It reminds me of the joke we used to say as kids, "Hey dad, I think you ran over the cat backing down the driveway. Pull forward to find out," only now, faced with the very real possibility that I have run over the dog or one of the cats, the thought of pulling forward and running over them again, isn't so funny. As I'm caught in a moment of indecision about if I should just keep driving down the driveway or get out to check on what I have driven over, my husband says, "Isn't today Wednesday? Tomorrow you need to remember to pack my shot."

"It's Thursday and yes, I packed the shot with the water bottles," I replied as my headlights flooded over the item lying in the driveway that I had driven over. Apparently, yesterday at some point someone had left a casserole on our side porch and some wild animals had dragged it onto the driveway and under our car. I mourned the loss of the casserole, but my grief deepened when I spied a package of chocolate covered graham cracker cookies, torn, crumpled and half eaten in the leftovers from last night's Raccoon Fiesta. I silently hoped that the raccoon's pants would't fit this winter, having over-indulged themselves on my cookies, baked especially for me, by the Keebler elves.

As we navigated onto the highway, I noticed that traffic was light, thankfully, so no repeat of yesterday. My husband dozed fitfully in the passenger's seat, wisely keeping his mouth shut about my lane choices.

When he finally opened his eyes, he turned to me. "Isn't today Wednesday. Don't forget to pack my shot tomorrow."

"It's Thursday and yes, I packed the shot with the water bottles."

I pulled up in front of the hospital. Handed him the lunch bag with the water bottles and shot.

"Today is Thursday," I say to him.

"Did you remember the shot?" he replies.

"If you mean the shot of Jameson whiskey for my morning coffee, ah no, I forgot that this morning. But thanks for reminding me. After all, it's Friday, so I might as well start the weekend early…"

Day 47: Flashback, June 1974: The sun pours down on us, like melted butter over popcorn, coating us in its warmth. A light breeze blows, just enough so the sun warming our skin is perfectly balanced.

This is the BEST DAY OF MY LIFE. I'm ten years old, on vacation in Wisconsin with my cousins, and my mom has decided swimming in the lake all week counts as bathing.

But this morning, we kids have stepped over a line with the moms; shrieking a bit too loudly, pushing and shoving a bit too hard. Our punishment is that the dads have to take us on a long hike, not returning until "someone has to be carried home."

My eldest cousin has put herself in charge, even though the dads are going with us.

"Little kids in the front. Single-file line. Hands to yourself. Don't leave the road. Don't run. Don't push. Don't touch anything," she keeps chanting, this endless mantra of rules, indicating that she's more adult than kid at twelve years of age.

We set off down the road, my cousin reviewing the rules periodically whenever someone steps out of line or tweaks an ear of the person in front of them. I soon shut her voice out, concentrating on the warmth of the sunlight on my sun-browned skin, so unlike the pale whiteness of all my cousins. I watch for birds, insects, and hope to spot a deer or fox.

The road stretches out in front of us, crystal blue skies giving the universe a feeling of vastness my ten-year-old mind can't grasp.

I see the marsh long before the others do. On the right-hand side of the road, down in a ditch, I spy what seems to be cattails. Each step draws us closer, each step pounds a thought into my brain.

Step. What would they feel like?

Step. Do they smell pretty like flowers?

Step. Can you eat them like the dandelions, tulips, and honeysuckle that I'm fond of?

Step. Would my dad get mad if I stepped off the road and picked some?

With each step taken, the cattails loom closer, beckoning me with their silent song of welcome. Swaying gently in the wind, it's as if I can hear some quiet song being sung by them each time they move. Back and forth, back and forth, they call my name, in a soundless tune, beckoning me forward to their home in the marsh. Something breaks inside of me. Some barrier comes down, shedding the mantra of rules my cousin is still chanting, and I break into a full run. My child's mind focuses on only one thing.

Cattails.

As I near the edge of the road where the cattails grow, I don't slow down, but rather dig even deeper, increasing speed. At the last minute, I shove off from the edge of the lane with both feet. My plan is to get enough speed and height to reach the cattails. Time freezes as I sail through the air. For a split second, I understand what a bird feels like when it is soaring through the air.

Of course, I haven't lived very long, so the fact that cattails grow in marshes hasn't occurred to me. As my feet enter the water, the land that should be there to meet me isn't. Down, down I go, plunging into swamp water up to my waist, my sneakers settling in muck. Millions of mosquitoes rise in celebration of a free lunch having come to their home.

None of this registers or matters to me. I am at one with the cattails, wrestling them, back and forth, trying to break their tough, reedy stalks, tearing my hands into a bloody mess. Not until I've ripped three stalks free from their bases does reality finally rush back in. I become aware that I'm standing in stinking water, with mosquitoes relentlessly draining my blood, and I feel the full horror of having broken every rule concerning this hike.

I look up at the road, into my father's unreadable face. He shakes his head, turns, and starts trudging back to the cabin. I struggle up the embankment, where I'm greeted by my cousin.

"You were NOT to leave the road. You were NOT to touch anything. You are in BIG trouble," she hisses.

I look her straight in the face. "I know, but I'm the only one going home with cattails."

I turn to follow the retreating back of my father, raise the cattails high like the Olympic Torch, and proudly march back to the cabin.

If fear has been preventing you from doing something on your bucket list, reconsider. You may have to leave the road, stand in stinking water and be eaten alive by insects, but when you accomplish a cherished goal, it will all have been worth it. Life is short. Really, really short. Don't wait for tomorrow, for it may never come.

If there are cattails on your walk in grace, make sure you stop and pick them.

Day 48: I made the commitment to a life of altruism at the age of ten. To serve mankind each and every day. Of course there's a long story about that day, but we will save it for another time. Suffice it to say, something happened in third grade to forever set me on that path.

Oh, I've strayed, many, many times. But each time, there would be a sign to get me back on track. Over the last few decades though, I really have tried to give my time and talents away as much as possible. If everyone will allow me to revisit our beloved pitchers from Day 7, then my approach for altruism has been this:

Each day, we wake up and we are like a pitcher overflowing with a golden liquid. It is our task as our day goes on, to pour out as much of the liquid as we can, spilling it on as many people as we possibly can. Each night, we should tumble into bed with an empty pitcher. The problem is, no matter how fast or furiously we pour out the golden liquid, there's still some left in the pitcher by our bed side when we close our weary eyes each night.

I do not ask for anything in return as I pour out my pitcher each day. It is simply enough to spread the golden liquid and feel at peace when I fall asleep. You will be splashed by the liquid from my pitcher and it is my hope that you will, in turn, start pouring out your pitcher even faster.

One of the amazing things about this path, is what is referred to as the Altruism Paradox. Simply stated, when someone has committed their life to giving everything away, more gifts come back to them than they could ever possibly give away.

This has been happening for the past few weeks for my husband and I. Gifts arrive almost daily, an outpouring of love, prayers, wishes, food, books, magazines, movies, it just goes on and on. We appreciate it all and are thankful to all the family and friends who have supported us through this arduous journey.

When cancer has finally fled our home, I will once again need to empty my pitcher onto others, paying them back for their kindnesses. Hopefully, by doing that, others will see the importance of finding someone who needs their help, support, love, or kindness. They will take the opportunity to share their time and talents, by pouring some of that golden liquid out of their pitcher. Splash around in it, celebrate it, create a beautiful flood of it, and ask for nothing in return.

Day 49: The first time I saw the face of depression, I was 5 years old. I stepped up to my mother's bedside, where she lay still, staring up at the ceiling, quiet, gentle tears rolling down the sides of her face. Despite my repeated attempts of patting her hand, and urgently saying "Mama," nothing could break the hold that her postpartum depression had on her. She simply could not respond.

My grandmother was the one who peeled me away from her bedside each time, muttering in her thick accent, "Today is Grey." As I was only five, this was taken as a literal statement. I looked to the windows, to the hot July sun baking the earth dry, and told her, "Nein, nein, nicht wahr" (no, no, not true).

"Kind weiss nicht!" she hissed (child, you don't know), propelling me away from my mother and out into the back yard. The dog beckoned, butterflies danced, clover tiara's were waiting to be made, and I lost myself in the sunshine, forgetting that somewhere close by, my mother lay in a bed, struggling to climb up from the deep hole she was in, where the day was perpetually Grey.

As I grew, I began to understand my mother's code for her depression. After all, in the '60s and '70s, no one talked about mental illness, at least not openly. Because my family did not believe in Western medicine, my mother did not receive any medical help either. So, to cope, she and her mother had developed a code long before, assigning colors to the day.

Pink Days, were glorious, spent outdoors by my side, weaving flowers into jewelry, humming, laughing, and celebrating the gifts that we had been given.

Blue Days were those tinged with sadness, not to the level of a Grey or Black Day, but ones where it was best to let her be, waiting to see which way she would swing.

Blue Days could become Pink Days or Grey Days depending on the moment when the swing would occur. When on the verge of turning the corner into the Grey Day room, she would sometimes unexpectedly stop and say, "You know, when your outlook on life is blue and sad, it just means you need to clean your windows," and that is exactly what she would do. For a long time, I really believed that cleaning away the grime on the windows, cleaned away the cause of her sadness.

I have lived a lifetime obsessively cleaning windows, and I still do. Last week, I cleaned mine, removing screens and storing them, allowing more sunshine into our home for the winter months. It also allowed me to feel a connection to my mother, long gone now, through an often shared activity that felt like she was with me. When the windows in my world are sparkling clean, it's a Pink Day for me and my outlook on life is brighter.

Right now, cancer is still in our home, coloring everything with shades of grey, blue, and black. Our emotions are tinged with levels of sadness, depression and despair, all day long, despite how positive we try to remain. Soon, very soon, we will be cancer free and our outlook through the window of life will be positive again, bringing the yellows and pinks back into our view.

Week 8: Everyone's Favorite OTC, Chocolate

Day 50: Twenty-four years ago today, my husband and I got married. He had a black eye (long story), my flowers were dead, my dress was ripped (longer story), and my hair had almost all fallen out the week before (longest story). We still got married. We didn't care.

We had been friends for years before we started dating and we dated for years before we even talked about getting married. It just seemed like some forgone conclusion, that at some point (sooner for my mother's sake) we should get married. So we did. The reception was an unforgettable party. I seem to be good at throwing parties.

I should have known that just getting married wouldn't appease my mother. She was convinced that she was born for one reason, and one reason only, to be a GRANDMOTHER. Shortly after the wedding, she took up the mantra, "When do you think you'll start having children?" Now it should be said that my mother almost never asked for anything for herself. For her to ask this one teeny, tiny thing of us seemed reasonable.

The problem was, after three years, seven infertility doctors, and uncountable daily treatments, everyone was stumped, and I still wasn't pregnant. My mother took the news that we were done with treatments and doctors stoically and then later in the day, casually asked about adoption. She wasn't going to give up.

I had though. I was emotionally, physically and spiritually exhausted. I was done. We wrapped our minds around the reality that we were never going to be parents. I was taking time to heal myself. But as the weeks passed, an unshakable flu finally sent me to the doctor's office.

I was 12 weeks pregnant. Some "flu!"

Our daughter was the first female born into my husband's family in eighty-seven years. Our son would follow three years later. We would officially be a family and we were done with infertility, pregnancies, and doctor visits. My mother was ecstatic in her new role as grandmother and the depression she had suffered with throughout my entire childhood lifted for the first time.

But soon after our son was born, I got the "flu" again. I called my mom, stunned about this unexpected pregnancy. Her response to me was simple, "God wants US to have this child" as if her role of grandmother was as important as ours as parents. It was as if this pregnancy was for her as much as it was for my husband and I.

She was right, of course. My beloved brother would be found deceased a few weeks later, from an undiagnosed genetic disorder. Days after the funeral, my mother called me, saying, "I'm having a Black Day. I want you to know the only reason I'm hanging on is because of your unborn child. I need to hold this baby, love this baby, and care for this baby." She had been right when she had said this baby was for US, all of us, for the pregnancy carried us all through the darkest of depressions and back into the light. After our second son was born, my mother loved him, just as she loved the other two. Deeply, devotedly, unconditionally, and remained in the Pink Days for eight months, which was when she was diagnosed with two forms of cancer.

Twenty-four years seems like a lot of time that my husband and I have had together. Then again it seems minimal when you hear of those who are celebrating twice that, but we managed to bring three amazing spirits into this world, weather all sorts of storms, and now we're dealing with a "little bit" of cancer in our lives. No biggie, we'll get through this, we always do.

Day 51: The PICC line came out yesterday. This line was placed in my husband's arm prior to the start of treatment so the chemotherapy medications could be delivered safely. It was also used to draw blood samples, preventing my husband from having to be stuck each week with needles. The PICC line also protects patients from chemotherapy drugs eating away at their arms if there's a leak. So, when it came out, we had mixed emotions.

True, it means my husband has a break from chemotherapy for a while and we don't have to do the daily flushing's which both of us dread and despise. But, it also means that any blood work next week will require a needle poke. My husband doesn't like needles. He really, really does not like needles.

And there will be blood work next week, because next Monday is when my husband goes in for the much anticipated follow up scans, blood work, and visits with the surgeon. An exciting day. A nervous day. A monumental day.

Many have asked over the past few weeks why surgery wasn't done immediately upon diagnosis. Why now, after three rounds of chemo? Because of the type of cancer my husband has, if it was removed when still "wet" it would have a greater chance of spreading. After a few rounds of chemotherapy though, it has formed a hard shell as a defense. It is more like removing a stone, than a mushy strawberry from his leg. In protecting itself, the tumor has helped the doctors ensure total recovery after surgery.

There is a nervous energy in our home right now because of the upcoming surgery. Will the doctor find clean lines around the tumor? Will he be able to get it all? Will the doctor ultimately have to amputate my husband's leg in order to save his life? Or if the leg is saved and only the tumor is removed, will my husband be able to walk normally after the surgery or will so much muscle mass be removed that his gait is affected? As much as I'm dreading the actual day of surgery, I wish it was just over.

We're definitely on the back side of the mountain now, making our way down. It feels good, it feels right. It also feels like we're picking up speed, racing toward that city called Remission. It looks like someone has left the lights on for us, a warm, welcoming sight. We have many friends there in Remission, so we can't wait until the day that we arrive. Soon, very soon.

***Day 52: Flashback, October 24, 1996:** A tsunami-sized wave of pain washes over me, blinding me, filling my ears so I am deaf to my surroundings. This is an ocean of pain I am lost in, some vast, endless sea of dark pain with no shore in sight. I slip under the surface, every cell of my body now consumed by the pain. Down, down... there is only pain and darkness here.*

"You're doing wonderful. Breathe, breathe." The nurse chants, her voice like a life-saver, thrown onto the surface of this hellish ocean. I reach out my hand, she takes it. "There, there, it's almost passed. Just a little bit longer."

The pain washes away from me, like the receding tide, and like a survivor lost at sea for days, I walk slowly up the shoreline, dripping with this watery pain. Each step taken, my vision becomes clearer, my mind more focused.

"Tell me again, why I agreed to this?" I ask, fiercely clinging to both her hands now.

"Because you are amazing. Very few women agree to this. You understood, when we asked you to do this, the importance of it. I know you are in a lot of pain, and we're very sorry for that, but what you are giving these students is an amazing gift and almost no one ever agrees to this. Especially when the students are all men."

A wave of pain, the size of the universe seizes me, blanking out my mind and senses, and I'm lost to her again.

"...and now that the epidural is in place," the doctor's voice booms somewhere behind me, "we can gently roll our patient onto her back please."

The medication starts to course through my body and my vision clears. As the pain melts away, I am able to finally participate actively in what is going on around me. The doctor in charge of teaching the class about anesthesia steps up to my side and takes my hand in his. He squeezes it and winks at me, a boyish grin spreading on his face. Behind him, seven pairs of anxious eyes peer over surgical masks at me. The men are nervous, a bit uncomfortable being here. "And that, is how we administer the perfect epidural," he says, finishing up his lecture and demonstration.

"That is a matter of definition," I say to the students. "The medical field will have you trained to believe that the perfect epidural is one in which the edge of the contraction pain is taken away, but the mother is still feeling enough labor pain to work through the contractions and advance the delivery. Women world-wide, would have you believe that the perfect epidural is one in which we can't feel anything from our waist down. Actually, some of

us would prefer no pain during childbirth from the neck down."

The students laugh and this eases their tension. This is the first time that all seven young men have ever been in a delivery room. Every minute of my third child's birth has been choreographed to look and feel like a normal delivery, while being a lecture on how to administer an epidural and deliver a baby. This is what my husband and I have agreed to. This is the gift that we have given these new upcoming doctors.

Labor progresses, my jokes start to fall away as the pain breaks through the epidural and makes talking difficult again. I try to keep a brave face for these students, but I cannot hide the pain from them, and I see reflected in their eyes the effect it is having on them. Each contraction infuses more compassion into them, and someday they will be better doctors and husbands for having been here with me. It makes the pain bearable.

The moment of delivery comes, and there's a tension in the room that wasn't there moments ago. My doctor steps up to me. The students gather at his back, crowding in like spectators at an arena. He looks at me and says to the gathered students, "All of you know that we have picked this amazing woman because she is willing to let you all

*participate here today. But, she was hand-picked by my
staff and I, because of who she is, and how she handled
herself at her last child's birth. Because of that, we're
going to show you something today, that rarely happens in
Western hospitals anymore." The doctor reaches a hand
toward me and helps me up.*

*I sit up, amid waves of pain striking me with a
fierce, repetitive force. I reach down, not to grab my legs in
the traditional form of delivery, but to guide my baby into
this world. I am going to deliver my child, assisted by this
doctor. I am going to bring life into this universe with my
own hands.*

And I do.

*The room erupts. Cheering, laughing, clapping,
tears flow down the students faces, leaving wet puddles on
their surgical masks. They crowd me, wanting to touch me,
see the baby. They shake my husband's hand, slapping him
on his back, thanking him profusely over and over for
allowing them to be present. We have given them an
incredible gift.*

*Having them share in the moment has given me an
incredible gift too. Knowing that women will be treated
more compassionately in the delivery room by these men,*

for they have seen how beautiful birth can be if a woman is given control of the situation.

We allow each student to take a turn holding our newborn son, allowing them to vote on the names we've chosen. Two argue amongst themselves, stating their cases for why they have voted for the name that they did. The good-humored banter among these young doctors is infectious and everyone joins the discussion. The baby is peaceful, serene; his eyes wide open, taking each of them in.

It feels like nothing bad will ever happen in our lives.

Life is beautiful.

Day 53: My husband's fever broke last night. Big, heavy sigh of relief. The doctors are mystified as to the cause, but they started him on a course of strong antibiotics a few days ago anyway. Apparently, he must have had a random bacterial infection somewhere in his body, for now his temperature has gone down and he's once again able to sleep peacefully. We're a few days away from surgery now and don't want anything to delay it.

It's warm outside. The sun is cresting over the eastern horizon. The windows are open, with the fresh smell of roving skunks wafting in. I wonder if they frequent our yard, still looking for casseroles and packages of Nutter Butter cookies. This leads to me wondering if the skunks and racoons would share the nightly feast if it was left out by a well-meaning friend who didn't want to disturb us by ringing the doorbell. Can racoons and skunks get along? Are they friends? I decide to get more coffee to clear my mind before I spend the whole day pondering the inter-relationships of nighttime foragers.

The street contractors might actually be finishing the paving of our road today, after what has seemed like months of ridiculous delays and incompetency's. Given this was supposed to be a seven-day project, even my predictions of it taking seven dog days, meaning forty-nine human days, was an underestimate.

I don't have one single car pool today (this is huge!). Which means, I can sit here in my Garfield pajama pants and my son's hand-me-up soccer shirt, drinking coffee, and eating cookies all day if I choose. Not that I don't do that when I do have carpool, as many days have been spent in these pajama pants and whatever random shirt I find in the laundry. It's just that I don't feel harassed or hurried about getting the day started.

The backpack actually did feel lighter this morning when I reached over to pick it up from the bedroom floor. Maybe the end is in sight and I'm starting to believe.

A close friend is in town and having dinner with us tonight. It will feel like something from our "old normal" lives and hopefully, cancer won't enter the conversation for the entire evening.

I hope everyone else also has an amazing, fever-free, sunshine-filled, and yes, skunk-smelling celebration of a day today. It's going to be a really good day.

Day 54: Flashback, October 2001: *I'm spending the day with my brother-in-law. No ordinary day, this one. No, it will be special. Just me and him. No spouses. No kids. No parents.*

I've had to line up three friends to cover all my carpools. Two co-workers to cover my shifts at work. I've jumped through some major hoops to make this day happen. I don't have any regrets about this, I've gladly done this when the family asked. In fact, I feel honored to be given this golden opportunity to spend an entire day with my brother-in-law, all by ourselves, with no one else around.

I arrive at his home, and let myself in. There's a note in the kitchen saying that canned soup is for lunch and to make sure he rests as much as possible. This is not how I have envisioned this day to be and I'm disappointed that my plans will have to be set aside, but the family's wishes need to be honored.

Softly, I make my way up the staircase and walk on padded feet toward his bedroom. It's dimly lit, quiet as a church at midnight. He's lying on the bed. I approach and take his hand in mine.

He is but a dried-up husk of a human being now. Cancer has ravaged his body from the inside out. His hand in mine feels claw-like, curled into a question mark, cold, clammy. His eyes slowly open and he turns to me.

"Hey" is all he is able to get out. I smile and wait, not responding. He musters all his energy, focuses it, and pulls what's left of his face into a smile. I exhale, not realizing I have been holding my breath all this time.

"Thanks for putting your life in my hands today and allowing me this time with you alone. I don't think I can begin to tell you how important and how special this is to me," I say holding back tears.

He squeezes my hand and smiles again.

I sit still, holding his hand and I start to talk. I start at the beginning, twenty years earlier, and tell of our adventures. The high points, the low points, all that has passed between us. We laugh, we cry, we smile. We celebrate the relationship we have had for more than two decades.

The time for lunch arrives. We've been talking about long-gone Marathon Bars, a favorite candy from the 1970's. I tell him there's canned soup for lunch and then tell him "That shit will kill you one day," which cracks us both up. Our laughter dies at about the same time when we both realize he only has days left to live.

I rise, to go heat the soup, but he pulls me back.

"I want a Marathon Bar for lunch instead," he pleads.

"Oh honey, they stopped making them years ago," I respond.

"If there is one person on this earth who can make this happen for me, it's you. Please." he asks.

"Be right back, bud," I say, half way out the door. I am under strict orders not to leave my brother-in-law alone for even five minutes. It's also expected that I will feed him the hated canned soup which contains vital nutrients essential for his fading body. Torn between what he wants and what the family wants, I throw caution to the wind and run off to the grocery store. I am back within twenty minutes.

"Got it!" I exclaim, walking back into the room. I'm holding a bag of candy behind my back. Not exactly Marathon bars, but this was the best I could find.

"You got a Marathon Bar?!?" he says. *"I knew you could do this for me!!!"*

"Well, they didn't exactly have any Marathon Bars, so I got chocolate covered caramels instead. My plan was to put them in the driveway in a line, run over them with my van, and smash them into a reproduction Marathon Bar. Or, you could save me the trouble and embarrassment of

driveway candy production and just eat the caramels outta this bag."

He laughs, moves his hand ever so slightly so it's open and ready and says, "Lunch!"

The rest of the afternoon is spent by his side, my brother-in-law slowly chewing caramels and listening to more of my stories.

Dinner time rolls around and we hear someone moving around downstairs. "Oh shit!" I spit out in a loud whisper, "I was going to throw that damn can of soup down the drain so it would look like you ate it. I was also going to eat all these candy wrappers to hide the evidence. I blew it and now there's going to be hell to pay." We laugh even harder than we have all day, semi-choking on chewy candies.

I get up to leave and he reaches for my hand. "Thank you for today. It's been the best day I've had in a really long time."

"Me too," I tell him. "Me too."

Our lives here are short, each day a gift. Make the most of every minute that you have been given.

And if you're in the neighborhood this weekend, stop on in. We'll line up chocolate covered caramels in the driveway and make our own reproduction Marathon Bars, better than eating canned soup. Probably should eat cookies for breakfast, dance in the rain, laugh in the face of adversity, throw your arms wide and embrace all that you have been given too. Spend time with one another, talk, play and celebrate.

Life is really short. Make the most of it.

Day 55: As a caregiver, I spend a lot of time sitting in waiting rooms. If I'm prepared, I bring a book to read, Christmas cards to address, or lists to compile. If I'm not prepared, I'm forced to sit and listen to the music that the doctor's staff has chosen.

There's the office that plays "theme" music depending on the day of the week. Wednesdays need to be avoided, as old country westerns twang overhead, making me feel over-dressed in khakis and sandals. Thursdays are no better, as Katy Perry and Rihanna duke it out for Most Overplayed Song of all time in the Bubble-Gum Pop division. I've never been on a Friday, but somehow I've convinced myself that it's probably Polka day and is best to be avoided.

This week though, I found myself stranded in an office which used an old, outdated CD player perched on the edge of a broken table as the music generator. Each time I've visited, the same CD is playing, as if this group of doctors is unable to afford even one other CD from Goodwill.

While being trained in classical piano as a child, particularly in memorizing the music, my teacher would always say, "Close your eyes while you listen to the music and visualize what you think the music means." I still do this, watching glorious movies in my mind while classical music dips and soars.

The problem, is that this also occurs when I listen to less-than-classy classical music. Thus, with no books or magazines (how could a doctor's office that cannot afford a second CD possibly afford magazine subscriptions?), I found myself focusing on the CD player and its monotonous drone. As usual, Track 5 which always seems to be cued up when I arrive at the office was playing, so I shut my eyes, and called up a visual of what the music was inspiring in me.

The track contained some harp chords, over-laid with what I perceived to be the sounds of a large beluga whale struggling to give birth. With no seaside epidural available, this poor mammalian mama thrashed, splashed and crashed her way through giving birth to a 250-pound behemoth of a baby. When Track 5 finally ended, I was left panting and exhausted along with the mother whale.

Track 6 immediately followed with a strange clanging of ominous church bells, ringing out the distinctive peals of a death toll. Despite all of mama whale's hard work, she has lost her life so that her newborn can live, clearly having not been attended to by modern medicine. The death knell grew, as minor organ chords chanted out a sad, tragic march and I felt the weight of the mother whale's sacrifice upon my shoulders. Somewhere in the back of the track, an odd trill in a major chord sprinkled in, and I realized that baby beluga had yet to realize that mommy had gone to whale heaven.

Silence then fell. I silently sent up a prayer that maybe this ancient CD player had finally played its last whale death march, but no. On the edge of my hearing, I realized with mounting horror that sea gulls were swooping down, as waves crashed on a distant beach. Track 7 brought the reality of the circle of life, for the arrival of these flying rats can only mean one thing. Poor mama whale had washed up on the beach, in her full postpartum glory. A brass section squealed out, signaling the sea gulls' excitement, and the party on the beach began. I felt slightly sick to my stomach.

I opened my eyes and realized there was another woman in the room with me, tapping her foot in rhythm, humming along to the music, oblivious to the carnage on the beach.

It's very possible I need more sleep than I am currently getting.

Day 56: We went grocery shopping today, in an attempt to appear normal to society and to ourselves. But, my husband currently has no hair anywhere on his body and his skin is a translucent, papery white vellum, showing all his veins and arteries like those long ago Invisible Man statues from our youth. These facts meant that, as much as we wanted and attempted to appear "normal," we were going to be gawked at by children and elderly men. We didn't care. It was just good to get out of the house and do something from our "old normal" lives.

We didn't really get very far into the shopping list before he became too tired and we had to leave. For a moment, I considered propping him up on a bench near the entrance and continuing with the list. I was desperate to get those items I felt we needed at home, but it felt wrong, putting my need for hair gel, white bread and Twizzlers before his need to lie down. I was sure it would also feel like leaving a child at the bus station with a note pinned to his jacket and $5 in his hand.

So we gave up, midway through the massive super center, walked to the checkout lane, purchased a jar of pickles, three bags of cotton balls, Cap'n Crunch ice cream, and what I had thought was a jug of laundry detergent. It turned out to be a bottle of "Sunny Sue's Sunny Shirt

Brightener." Super glad my shirts will be fluorescing and glowing, but now I'm struggling with whether I can wash my Garfield the Cat pajama pants with the Super Bright Sunny Stuff or if Garfield will implode from all of the super-amazing brightening molecules.

On the drive home, I concentrated on the positive aspects of the trip. The fact that my husband had gotten out of the house, going somewhere other than a doctor's visit or trip to the hospital, was a plus. The fact that we had spent some much needed time together, doing something from our old routine was another plus. The fact that the first thing into our cart had been ice cream, call that a double plus. Then there is the Super Sunny Spectacular Shirts we will all be sporting for the next few weeks.

I decided that it had been a great trip after all, a good day, one that should be celebrated. Score one point for the home team, zero for cancer. We celebrated by eating ice cream for dinner.

Week 9: Ordinary Is the Best Kind of Extraordinary

Day 57: Tomorrow we spend the day at the hospital for my husband's follow-up scans, blood work, and doctor's appointments. It will be a long, exhausting day. It will also be stressful and emotional. But, we will finally find out how much the chemotherapy and radiation have worked and we will leave with a surgery date set, knowing that the tumor will be removed soon.

It seems like years ago, not months, that my husband found the mass in his leg. Yet, here we are close to another monumental milestone in his recovery. Today we will rest, relax, and cheer our hometown favorite football team on toward another victory (hopefully!). Tomorrow we will celebrate our own victory.

I wish I could individually thank all the wonderful friends and family who have walked besides us on this journey toward Remission. This is a walk that should never be taken alone, so we are grateful for all the amazing, wonderful, loving people who have surrounded us, strengthened us, supported us. When I reflect on where we were and how far we have come on this journey, I am always overwhelmed by everyone's support.

The sun has yet to rise this morning, but I can already tell it's going to be a great day. One of our cats, Catzilla, is sleeping quietly on my desk, done shredding all the important papers I have left there. The other cat, Catitude, is wrestling with our dog, Dog Gone, in some furry, four-legged version of semi-professional wrestling that is only seen on Pay-Per-View. I'm almost done picking coffee grinds out of my teeth and I have no intention of getting out of my Garfield pajama pants today. Perhaps it's serendipity or maybe just plain old dumb luck, but last night in my exhaustion, as I was getting ready for bed, the shirt I grabbed from the laundry basket is the one my husband gave me when we were first dating. Actually, if I think about it, I probably grabbed it as it was glowing brightly, having been through the "Sunny Sue's Sunny Shirt Brightener" yesterday and it caught my eye. Either way, it is the perfect shirt, to start this important week.

Faded robin-egg blue, with smatterings of bleach stains from a long-ago cleaning frenzy, the message still is readable in the peeling, white iron-on letters.

"Go Forth and Succeed"

It's going to be a really, really good week.

Day 58: Back from a day at the hospital. This was the day when we got all the follow-up results from the treatments.

The tumor has not shrunk, but it wasn't supposed to shrink. By staying this size, the doctor can pop out a "walnut" (his words) instead of trying to scoop out a soupy mix of shrunken tumor cells. So, it's really a good thing.

Surgery won't be for another week now, later than anticipated. This gives my husband a longer time to recover from radiation and chemotherapy, so he'll be stronger going into surgery. The surgeon truly believes that, despite having to remove a sizable portion of my husband's thigh muscles around the tumor, he will be up and walking the day after surgery. He's even predicted that my husband will not have a limp. I'm relying on his thirty-one years in surgery and accepting his opinion on faith.

Beyond that, I've now sat here for fifteen minutes trying to come up with something witty or clever, and all that has come through is that I am beyond exhausted at this very moment in my life. The backpack should be feeling lighter, but somehow today has left me doubled over under its weight. At the same time, I feel exhilarated because of something the oncologist said while in her office. She looked at us and said, "After surgery, you should think of yourself as cancer free."

I guess people are right when they say the Best Things in Life are Free.

Cancer free.

Day 59: A friend once told me that pain was necessary in life. That it was a good thing to experience. That she actually felt sorry for people who had never experienced spiritual, social, or emotional pain from some catastrophic event.

At the time, I thought she was crazy.

But now that I'm older, I understand what she meant. Pain takes you to a place where you rarely, I hope go. You definitely don't go there willingly. It's like you're dropped from a helicopter, into a vast, endless Sea of Pain. Some people flounder around, screaming out for someone to rescue them. Panicked, hysterical, unable to help themselves, needing assistance to find their way back home. They are the ones to whom we need to reach out, to touch, to hold, and to bring home to a safe harbor.

Others quietly tread water, swishing around in the pain, biding time until they bump up against the shoreline, plodding slowly up the sandy beach toward recovery, dripping wet with residual pain.

Then there are those who, when thrust into the unrelenting Sea of Pain, hit the water and immediately start swimming. They pull with hard, strong strokes fighting against the waves of pain pushing against them. These folks don't know in what direction to swim, they just know that they don't want to spend one more minute in that vile water than they have to. They emerge on the beach victorious, shaking away the watery drips of pain like a wet dog.

In the end, it doesn't really matter how we act in the Sea of Pain. Only what we do once we've reached the beach and found solid ground under our feet. What we do with our experience in that Sea of Pain, that makes a difference.

We can allow the pain to make us a bitter person, hardening our heart to others who are experiencing the same pain. Or we can choose, by attitude, to allow the pain to make us a better person. Allow it to soften our hearts to the plight of those still struggling against the crashing surf. We are better people if we use our experience in the Sea of Pain as a guideline for helping others to swim toward the shore and help them once they are back on steady ground.

The choice is ours. Bitter or better. You choose.

Day 60: Who takes care of the caregiver?

This question always comes up eventually, when I'm in this role. It's a multifaceted question really. It implies that the caregiver is not taking care of her- or himself. Which is usually true. Given the pain, suffering, exhaustion and chaos of the moment, the first brick tossed out of the overburdened backpack to lighten the load, is usually self-care.

It also implies that someone should be the caregiver to the caregiver. But then, who takes care of the caregiver who is caring for the caregiver?!? Where does that network end?

The answer is, it doesn't. At least, not in the town I live in. Here, the network is a vast spider-web, cast over the entire city, where caregivers scurry along silken strands, stopping from point to point, to drop off meals, run carpools, kiss boo-boos, deliver much-needed hugs, scrub windows, and tend to whoever needs tending. If you happen to be a bug, accidentally stuck in our web, we scramble up to you, spinning a gossamer blanket of love and kindness around you, then tend to you until you're rested enough to be on your way.

I've spent twenty-one years in this town, running around the web, caring for those who needed caring for.

Now, I'm a caregiver in need of caring for and the town has responded. Beautifully, others beyond the city limits have also responded, so that this gossamer blanket that has been spun and holds me tight is sturdy, supportive, and loving.

Soon, I won't need this blanket. I'll shed it like a butterfly emerging from a cocoon. I'll return to the web to scurry about helping those who need *my* assistance. It will feel good to get back to helping others. It will feel good to not be so dependent on others too.

But for now, it's just nice to rest in the peaceful bliss of this amazing blanket and know that my family is being taken care of.

Day 61: I woke with the word BELIEVE stamped on the inside of my forehead.

I laid there for a long time, trying to figure out why this word was on my mind. What was the significance behind this being the first thing I should think about upon waking? What was the message my subconscious mind was sending up into my waking brain?

It took me some time, but I finally came up with two things. My first thought was, even though it was before 4 a.m., I was not going to fall back asleep. Might as well get up and start the day.

My second thought was, maybe this was just a gentle reminder of the past sixty days.

BELIEVE you can bear the load of the brick-heavy backpack of troubles, even when you struggle under its immense weight with every fatigued-filled step.

BELIEVE that the pitcher of living water is still here, overflowing with rich gifts, meant to be poured out each day, even when your only contact with the outside world is through a computer.

BELIEVE you are exactly where you are meant to be in life, even if it's not where you would choose to be, given a choice.

BELIEVE that each step taken is in the right direction, no matter how dark the forest, how scary the path, how painful the journey.

BELIEVE that you can overcome any obstacle in your way, you just have to keep working at it.

BELIEVE.

Catzilla was again sleeping on my hip this morning when I awoke. The difference being, it was my right hip, the non-deformed hip, so no pain shot through me when I stood up. It might mean a pain-free day today, one where great, momentous things are accomplished. Or, it might mean a typical, messy, chaotic day, just a hip pain-free one. Either way, it's the day I am meant to have, the kind of day I was meant to travel.

I just have to BELIEVE it's the right one for me.

I also BELIEVE there are some cookies downstairs in the pantry.

And I BELIEVE they were meant to be eaten for breakfast.

May today be what you BELIEVE it should be.

And may you BELIEVE in yourself.

Day 63: Yeah, I know, where is Day 62? Did we have such a terrible, no-good, awful Day 62 that I couldn't write about it? Was Day 62 spent struggling just to breathe and survive, so no writing could occur? Did we receive some horrendous news about my husband's health on Day 62 that it caused a cataclysmic spiral down into that lowest level of Hell that we haven't reached yet?

No. Day 62 occurred and there was no bad news other than my computer holding me hostage. The power supply went out on my computer for the umpteenth time yesterday and I was without technology. That's not to say, there wasn't technology in my home and surrounding me, it's just that the computer was about the only thing I needed to use, besides the coffee maker that required electricity.

I only sort of missed it. Still, I became obsessed with getting it fixed, for fear that everyone would start flooding my home eventually, wanting to know where we were at with everything and how we were doing. As if a lack of computer connection would cause everyone to jump to the conclusion that I had been forced to enter into the Witness Protection Program and I had destroyed my computer before I fled. My imagination sometimes fills in the blanks with a level of drama that makes daytime soaps look boring and stilted.

But really, yesterday wasn't anything that exciting. Day 62 was just this: it was normal. It was every day. It was a ho-hum, run of the mill, typical American day in our lives.

It was really, really, really wonderful.

My husband is at a point in the recovery, awaiting his surgery date, where we can have people stop in (and boy have they!) and visit. Their comments are almost universally the same, "You look really good. I mean, you look really GOOD."

Damn, ya gotta love the sound of that.

We still love trips to Disney, airboat rides through the Everglades, parasailing in Key West, beignets in New Orleans, adventures, excitement, and thrills.

But nothing, I mean NOTHING, beats an average, nothing happened, no one got sick, regular kind of day. Day 62 was glorious.

Week 10: The New Captain of This Ship is Capt'n Crunch

Day 64: I got home from work and found the kitchen filled with cereal boxes, plates of cookies, and banana bread. I asked my son who had dropped everything off. I'm not sure why I bothered. He's a teenager. He's a boy. Need I say more?

"Who brought all the food for us," I asked.

"Some lady," he replied.

"Did you know her?"

"No."

"Umm, help me out here, what did she look like? Was she short or tall?"

"Dunno."

"Was she heavy or thin?"

"Dunno."

"What color was her hair?"

"Maybe red curly hair. Or it could have been dark and straight. Not sure."

"Anything else you can tell me about her? Old, young? Freckles, wrinkles? Any accents? Did she have glasses on? I need to know who to thank, and that's not much to go on."

"Um, she might have been tall. No, maybe she was as short as you. I think she was wearing a red sweater? But it could have been a blue sweatshirt."

Scratching my head, trying to maintain my temper, "Is there really nothing you can tell me that would help identify who dropped off all this food?"

"She was driving a silver grey Volkswagen Jetta S, I'd say around a 2008 or 2009, well kept, few dings, mid-range engine, four-door with manual transmission, custom paint job, tone-on-tone, and the sunroof was open."

Bingo.

Day 65:

I am the highest mountain. Soaring forever into the sky, piercing clouds, losing my crest in an unattainable stratosphere. You have trod my well-beaten path, struggling to conquer me, pushing yourself beyond human endurance to gain my peak. Some have failed, others have achieved. I help no one.

I am the fiercest of fires. The hottest of flames, consuming all in my path. Scorching, searing, and burning with an internal rage that cannot be contained. Mine is to destroy, leaving nothing in my wake. To be touched by me is to feel heat so blinding, you are hollowed out, left cold and empty inside.

I am the darkest of nights. No stars or moon to illuminate the path. Blind trust is to be your only guide this night. Wandering with outstretched hands, groping, feeling along, this is to know loneliness, lost in the complete blackness, no sense of time or space.

I am the deepest of oceans. Bottomless, cold, consuming, no island to rest upon, your choices are to swim or sink, forever lost in my clutches. You are mine and the siren song heard far away, is only your own voice resonating in your head, whispering to give up, give in, and give over to me.

I am the vast and looming desert, my endless sands reaching to the horizon and beyond. My heat leaches all power from your cells, draining you of energy, hope and conviction. With no oasis in sight, you must continue to place one foot in front of the other, toil through my hell, for to stop is to admit defeat, to be emptied of all life.

I am cancer.

Day 66:

We are warriors. Storming up the mighty mountain, forging up its steep precipice, never resting, never pausing, always climbing toward the summit where victory lies. We join hands and help each other reach the apex. No one climbs this mountain alone.

We are warriors. Dousing the flames, pushing back the fires that rage unattended. Water, chemicals, powders and sheer will; we use all at our disposal to put out this mighty flame. We join hands and help each other vanquish the flames. No one battles this fire alone.

We are warriors. Fighting the darkest night, shining our light in every corner, pushing back the heavy darkness that consumes us. We trudge ever forward, spreading our beacon of hope, this lantern of love, devouring the dark and reclaiming the light. We join hands and help each other forward through the never-ending blackness. No one walks in this darkness alone.

We are warriors. Battling the deepest ocean, conquering swells, surviving the waves, swimming ever toward the shoreline. The ocean endeavors to swallow us whole, taking us down into its murky depths, but we wage a war, claiming victory as we walk onto the shore. We join hands and help each other to dry land. No one swims in this ocean alone.

We are warriors. Conquering the driest of deserts, moving forward through heat and despair, sickness and sorrow. Each step taken, brings us near the victory. We feel the internal fire that rises through the desert and envelopes us, draining our energy, but we continue on. We join hands and help each other into the shade. No one treks over this desert alone.

We are warriors. We are cancer survivors.

Day 67: Each year I sew about 100 Christmas stockings for the children in town who are from families that are struggling economically. I start in May, sewing in fits and starts, sometimes going for weeks without touching the sewing machine, but somehow I get them done by the first weekend in November.

Not this year. Cancer came, stealing away our everyday lives and leaving in their place some spasmodic, herky-jerky semblance of normalcy. I've tried going into the art room over the past few months and even tried sitting down at the machine long enough to lose myself in the reds, greens and golds of the Christmas season. I just can't stay focused. Somehow, I sit there idle, until some other emergency or task calls me away.

It's as if, the moment someone you love is diagnosed with cancer, you are forced to step out onto the big Cancer Stage of Life. Once the curtain goes up on this scene, the Grand Master Puppeteer, Cancer, starts jerking the strings connected to your arms, legs, mind and free will, maniacally tossing you all about this dismal, hateful stage. You have no control over your day, you must obey the Puppet Master whether you want to or not.

You go places on this stage that you fear, that you loathe, that make you sad and desperate. You're pulled from one end to the other, while the Puppet Master's gravelly voice floats down to you, "You are mine. You must do as I bid you." You pray for an intermission.

There is none.

Don't worry, the children here in town will not miss out because the Cancer Grinch has stolen Christmas. Friends came through for me, picking up the slack and sewing the stockings. It's just that I'm looking forward to the curtain falling on this tragedy that's being played out and the new production of "Cancer Free Forever More," debuting shortly. I've already got front row seats for that production.

I can't wait until the curtain is raised on that show.

Day 68: Our street is finally finished. Asphalted, lines striped, curbing in place, it feels like such a gift to be able to pull into our driveway, right up to the door. It also seems like a million years ago I was slogging through the gravel pit to retrieve much needed IV supplies from the truck parked at the church parking lot down the street.

The IV pole is actually put away, in a dark corner of our closet for the time being. Not that we're done using it. We will definitely need it once chemotherapy resumes after the surgery. But for now, I don't want it out as a constant reminder of where we were a few weeks ago. I don't want to enter my bedroom or the living room and see it standing there, like an insulting exclamation point, proclaiming, "Cancer! Here! Now!"

The gauze pads (Note to self: check expiration date to be sure they are still compliant), saline fluid bags, tape, hemostats, gloves, and masks, are also shoved into the closet. This detritus of treatment is also a constant statement that there is illness here, lurking somewhere within one of us. Out of sight, out of mind, has become my driving force for allowing me to wear the cloak of denial through ridding my house of this evidence. Even if it's only for a few weeks.

Last night I made dinner for our family too. A small baby-step back toward our normal lives of the past. True, it was only macaroni-and-cheese from the box, a can of green beans heated in the microwave and some chicken that I baked too long and could only be described as "Chicken Jerky." But it felt wonderful, truly marvelous, to do a "normal" mom-thing again. Thankfully, no one made any negative comments about the meal, instead, choosing to quietly slip the "De' Hydrate Chicken" to the dog under the table.

When the dog vomited up the mess later on the carpet, it had a weird feeling of normalcy too. I am definitely tired of cleaning up vomit, but this was a reaction of consuming too much badly cooked chicken, and not because of some dreadful disease like cancer. I actually whistled and hummed while I cleaned it up, until I caught sight of my one son shaking his head at me and whispering, "Gone. Over the edge. Lost it," to his brother.

Yeah, definitely feels like the old normal again.

Day 69: I passed the Mystery Machine the other day on my way to the grocery store. I'm not making this up; I honestly passed a full-sized van, painted exactly down to the last detail as a replica of Scooby Doo's Mystery Machine.

I had a strong urge to pull a U-turn and follow the van figuring they were on their way to a case only "those meddling kids" could solve. Let's face it, solving the mystery of the Swamp Beast or the Wailing Walla Walla was more interesting than price-comparing the cost of granola bars or analyzing the ingredient list on the Swiss Rolls Package to ensure that they qualify as a breakfast food.

But, practicality got the better of me and I continued to the store. I did ponder how beautiful life was in the Scooby Doo world. How the underlying optimism each week was why we were so drawn to it as kids.

The "Gang" never changed their outfits. They were so comfortable in their self-esteem that they showed up to every mystery in a white shirt with ascot, short orange dress with knee socks, purple vogue dress, and an ugly green t-shirt. They clearly sent us all a message that said, "Hey, it's not how you're dressed, it's how you behave that matters." The fact that they never seemed to have any friends, probably because their clothes smelled so bad from 365 consecutive wearings, somehow escaped our young minds.

They had a cool dog that could communicate beyond the simple tail-wagging, tongue-lolling level that modern-day dogs have evolved to. Scooby didn't need money, accolades, or fame, he simply needed Scooby snacks, those undefined treats that made Scooby mad for more. Given that this cartoon ran during the 1960's and 1970's, it probably should have crossed our minds that maybe the Scooby snacks were baked with hash or opium, thus making Shaggy lusting after them forever too. Somehow this fact always escaped our naive minds.

For some reason, the "Gang" never got paid, nor ever needed money. They were simply happy to travel the country, solving mysteries for free, thrilled to help out. Perhaps the Mystery Machine was solar powered, never needing fuel and the "Gang" lived on those hallucinogenic filled Scooby Snacks. Velma, Fred and Daphne, never seemed to need food, while Shaggy and Scooby could never get enough.

Then there was the greatest mystery of all. Where were the parents of these kids? In an age before cell phones, even practical Velma never worried about finding a pay phone to check in with her mother or father. These five had simply been given carte blanche to travel parts unknown by parents that must have been the coolest on the planet. Today, modern parents can't make it fifteen minutes after dropping their kids off before texting to check on them.

Perhaps if I pass the Mystery Machine again, I won't think twice and I'll turn around and follow them. I already practically live in my Garfield the Cat pajamas 24/7 anyway, so I've got the fashion side of the Scooby Crew down. I would just need to hone my detective skills, which now that I think about it, given the level of splatter patterns constantly being created by the cats and dog, I probably have more Sherlock Holmes talents under my belt than I realize.

Should the Weinermobile come to town, I'll be first in line to sing the "I Wish I Was an Oscar Meyer Weiner" song, off-key, just to get the whistle. No amount of price-comparing on peanut butter or tube socks could distract me from that.

What a great country America is!

Day 70: I'm something of a Martha Stewart when it comes to Christmas decorations. Our crawl space contains thirty-seven bins which hold all the decorations. I'm not talking itty-bitty bins, I'm talking huge, give-me-a-hand-with-these bins.

We start the day after Thanksgiving. Our porch and exterior take two days. There's a theme, usually lasting for about five years. We're in year three of the "Dr. Seuss' Magical Christmas" theme on our porch. People pull up as we're having dinner, stop their cars and take photographs of the porch. The weird thing is, I really don't even think it's all that great. The only thing I can figure is, I'm the only nut-case whose porch is decorated in magenta, aqua, orange, purple and red. You just don't see that every day. Certainly not at Christmas.

The rest of the house gets transformed in about six days. Not ordinary days. I wake up between 2 and 4 a.m. and plow through decorations. Moving, fussing, cleaning, redecorating, I keep doing and re-doing, until everything is in its place. Then I move everything again, because something just doesn't feel right. I drive everyone in my family crazy. I even drive myself crazy.

This year it occurred to me that my husband is having surgery in mid-November and he will have a honking huge wound in his leg, preventing him from moving bins, hanging lights and lifting boxes when we go to decorate.

Uh, oh.

I thought about not doing the exterior and cutting back on the interior. That thought lasted for about five minutes before I squashed it like a vile bug crawling up my arm.

So, last Friday, my husband got up on the roof and hung Christmas lights. Yup, it was November 3rd. A friend chastised me for sending my "sick" husband up there when he should have been "resting" for his upcoming surgery. Told me that I clearly wasn't thinking straight in sending him up there to hang decorative lights and risking a fatal accident should he have fallen. I didn't know how to respond to her, as he "risks" his life every year hanging the lights on the eaves and why was this year any different? Just because there was a tumor in his leg, this was supposed to prevent him from getting up on a ladder? What I really wanted to explain to her was how the process of decorating our home was part of our "old normal," something we both desperately missed and that while we were out hanging garlands and wiring glass balls to handrails, we felt, well, normal. We felt, cancer-free.

It's not that I wanted to rush the season. I didn't want to be part of the madness gripping America. Stores decorated the day after Halloween for Christmas, thus effectively wiping Thanksgiving off the American calendar. But, I didn't want to miss our home being decorated for Christmas either. I guess, if I'm honest with myself, what I feared in not decorating, was that it would feel like cancer had won another round in this vicious battle. That we would have taken one more giant step away from "old normal" and given into "new normal." In the battle against our arch-nemesis cancer, decorating that first weekend in November felt like a minor victory. If nothing else, it felt like self-preservation.

So, my apologies to everyone in town, who had to drive by my home and see the Christmas decorations up early. This was the only workable compromise that I could find.

Who knows, I may use this as an excuse to leave them up until April and drive everyone crazy. Magenta, aqua, orange, purple and red look great for Easter, don't they?

Week 11: That's Gonna Leave a Scar

Day 71: Sometimes the days before surgery are worse than the actual day of surgery. Waiting, wondering, worrying, wanting it to just be over.

My husband's surgery is now a few days away. So very close to when we will be finally cancer free. Keeping busy during this per-surgical waiting period has been difficult, as our minds tend to drift to the upcoming procedure. We wrestled with Christmas decorations today, trying to keep our minds off of next Tuesday. The tree on the porch is up, some garland is strung and when we went out earlier, we discovered that a number of our neighbors had taken advantage of the mid-60's mild weather and decorated too. We didn't feel so bad.

Tonight, we went to the annual Turkey Raffle. This was the 62nd year that this has been done in our town. It used to be the Turkey Shoot, but like everything else in our society, we had to become politically correct, so the name was changed a few years back. At least now my phone doesn't ring each year with some irate citizen wondering why I'm down at the fire station shooting ninety poor, innocent turkeys. As if my aim is good enough to even shoot one of those poor birds.

No, they arrive dead, plucked and frozen. We never have shot one over there that I'm aware of. As we look forward to this event each year, it's nice that it falls during a point in my husband's treatment that we are able to attend. We had to leave a bit early, but being out amongst friends and hearing their encouraging words was worth the exhaustion. If not for my husband's lack of hair and mustard yellow tinged skin, this would have felt like our "old normal" lives again. It was still good to get out of the house though. To be out among the living.

We'll continue to do typical, average day-to-day things to keep our minds occupied tomorrow. But tomorrow we will be two days away from being cancer free, instead of three. It's truly the little things in life that make each day extraordinary.

Day 72: The power supply went out on my computer again today. It's become an almost daily event now and I realized that I don't miss it when I have no connection to the world of technology.

It made me wonder about things we miss out on because we're so caught up in cyber-space.

I remember sitting on a porch swing under a grape arbor one day with my younger brother. We were sipping cold beers, after a long, hot day of slinging asphalt. Filthy, sweaty, exhausted, my mom found us, both underage, drinking these cold drafts stolen from our father's stash. She went quietly back into the house, we presumed to get our dad, so he could beat us black and blue. Instead, she emerged with her camera and snapped our picture. Smiling, she went back inside without speaking a word.

I remember catching tadpoles in the back fields of the farm property behind our home each spring. After raising them into frogs, we would let them go, laughing as they hopped maniacally to get away from us. No thanks ever given for the countless flies we caught and fed to them.

I remember making clover chains into tiaras, necklaces, bracelets, whatever we fancied and wearing them for the day. When the clover was depleted, we would use dandelions, our hands stained tarry black from their milk. Eating tulip stems, carrots coated in mud, and honeysuckle flowers, finishing off the meal with raspberries and cold, metallic-tasting water from the hose.

I remember catching banana spiders by the thousands, filling canning jars with them. At the end of each day, we would release them, so we could fill the same jar with lightning bugs later that night.

There are no fields of clover now, herbicides have killed them off. Floods are controlled by retention ponds so tadpoles are born somewhere far off. I'm long past the legal age to drink, so the thrill of a stolen beer is a distant memory. Thankfully, I no longer sling asphalt during the summer months.

It's okay though. I have my memories of these moments and more, and all it takes to bring them back is for the power supply to fail on my computer. Which will probably happen again soon!

Day 73: My husband had surgery today at 10:45 a.m. This meant that, when we woke this morning, we were only a few hours away from being cancer free.

It seemed like this had been a long, endless journey at times; at other times like a too-fast roller coaster. Now, we are almost down to the base of the mountain and recovery is in sight. We can actually see glimpses of remission too and it's a beautiful sight.

When the surgeon emerged after the operation, he told us it went well, then whipped out his cell phone to show us the pictures of the muscles and tumor that had he had removed from my husband's leg. My father-in-law blurted out that it looked like a steak. This combined visual with voice over, was enough that I may have to become a vegetarian. The relief felt by all of us in the room was almost palpable, despite the fact that somewhere in post-op my husband was struggling to shrug off the anesthesia.

As there were problems in post-op, staff were refusing to let me go back to see my husband. After almost four hours, I started to throw a fit in the waiting room. To quiet me down, they finally granted my son and I permission to go back to post-op. Finding my husband hunched over in bed, vomiting violently, I blew a gasket. Luckily for the staff, when I become angry, instead of raising my voice, I lower it to a slow, menacing snarl, that my children have described as "stops you dead in your tracks, scary." After pointing out to them, that the pain medications they were giving my husband were actually hurting him by making him nauseous, changes were made. Within an hour he had stabilized and was moved upstairs. This was truly the very first time we experienced anything less than exceptional in the care he had received at this hospital, so I really shouldn't have been all that upset.

By midnight, he was finally settled in and I left with my sons and father-in-law for home. The drive on the expressway was beautiful, very few cars on the road at this time of night. But as we neared home, I realized the reason that the night seemed so beautiful. It wasn't the stars overhead in the clear, crisp cold night sky or the empty expressway void of stressful congestion.

No, the night was beautiful, because now we were cancer free.

Day 74: Flashback, November 14, 1998: *I'm running late for tonight's event. I've been planning this "Celebration of Women" event for months now, and as usual with small kids at home, time always seems to be missing from my day, leaving me late to everything of importance. As I'm looking for my keys, the phone rings.*

I really don't have time to talk to whoever is calling. I take a step toward the door and the phone rings again. Something pulls me back, making me turn on my heel, grab the phone and answer a rushed hello, trying to imply to the caller that I just don't have time for this.

It's my close friend from high school, calling about our mutual best friend, the one in the last stages of her battle with breast cancer. "Hey, it's me love," he starts out, and I can hear the sadness in his voice before he even speaks the next words. "I'm calling because she isn't going to make it through the night and I thought you'd want to know." This dear friend starts to sob, fracturing my world.

"No" is all I'm able to say, words escaping me, all my energy draining away, leaving me feeling like an empty soda can lying abandoned on the side of the road.

"She's fought the good fight. She's been brave and heroic, but now she's weary of the battle and she'll be at peace soon," he says.

"No" leaks from me again, my vocabulary reduced down to this one word.

He continues to talk, but my hearing is gone. My vision has dimmed and my voice gone mute. Inside, my brain rages, screaming in a voice filled with rage, fear and sorrow. This is wrong, my mind yells, this is an older woman's cancer. This shouldn't be happening to women my age and most certainly not to my best friend. She's only thirty-five! This is not fair. This is not right. This is a nightmare, one that soon, very soon, I'll wake from, and she will be there. Healthy with all her hair and we'll break open a box of Frango mints and a bottle of tequila, and laugh until we cry about this weird dream we've had where she got sick in her early thirties with breast cancer.

But I am awake and she is in the last hours of her battle with this monster, cancer, in her home, thousands of miles away. Too far for me to get to her in time, so I am forced to stay here and slap a smile on my face, like some grotesque Halloween mask, walk out the door and attend the event tonight. Pretending that everything is okay in the world and that it's wonderful to be a woman.

And that is what I do.

I show up to the event, smiling, greeting everyone, welcoming them. I swallow the sour bile, rising in the back of my throat, and get through the evening. I'm actually even doing okay, the entertainer I've hired for the night providing an amazing array of funny, provocative, original songs, that have been a beautiful diversion.

But then it's all over. Women are thanking me, praising the singer, laughing, joking, and smiling as they file out. The mayor is one of the last in line, and when she grabs my hand, says, "Thank you so much for this great evening. Being a woman is the greatest gift and it was so nice to be reminded about that!"

It's the proverbial straw on that overburdened camel's back. The anger, sadness, despair, exhaustion that have been living in the back of my throat and mind all night, burst forth, flooding through me like a poisonous river.

"No it's not! My best friend is in the last few hours of her life right now, having lost her battle with breast cancer. I hate this disease, and it's not fair that we women have to deal with this, given all the other crap we have to put up with!"

The room grows quiet, the few remaining women turning toward us, silently assessing the situation.

The mayor pauses, for the merest of moments, then the wisdom of her years, rains down on me like a gentle

snow fall, quieting my tears. "You have such pain right now
and a lot of anger. But that's part of being human. It's a
part of being a woman and if we never experienced any
pain, then when we found joy, we would never appreciate
it. In time, when the pain ebbs, you need to focus on what
your friend meant to you, but more importantly, you need to
focus on what your friend meant to others too. You'll see,
that her battle was meant to be fought at this young age for
a reason."

So, for me, my dear friend, you were beautiful eyes
and an amazing smile, a dry, quick wit, an uncooked
cheesecake the night before my wedding, matching
pajamas, dinner and a musical in the city for your birthday
each year, a six pack of beer to ease the pain when a horse
bit the crap out of my shoulder, rainy days in your VW Bug
with no defroster, and someone I could always count on to
have my back.

For others my friend, you were an amazing example
of how to walk in grace when you were dealing with
cancer, and how to do it with humor, dignity, strength, and
love daily.

A beautiful lesson to me and all those around you,
each and every day, and one I have never forgotten. My
dear friend, you were one of the early guides, who helped

me find my way back to the path, when I had wandered too far. You were one of the early guides, love.

Day 75: So, radiation is over. Surgery is over. Chemotherapy is half over. But, there's still work to be done on this road to recovery and remission.

My husband came home yesterday from the hospital, with a 9" long incision in his leg. Dressings need to be changed (EWWWW), he has a drain in the leg that needs to be emptied three times a day (DOUBLE EWWWWW) and he lost enough muscle tissue that he cannot lift his leg, making navigation in our four story home interesting.

He is doing well though. Eating, sleeping, minimal pain, we are at a good place on this road to recovery and remission. We're just not quite there yet. It's as if we are on the back side of the mountain, hiking down. The steps taken are easier, the breathing not so labored, and the destination, that beautiful city called Remission is within sight. We just have a little farther to go on this journey.

We're close enough to the town of Remission now, that I can see they're already hanging the decorations for the party that we'll throw. It's going to be amazing. I'll make sure everyone's pitcher is full and that there are plenty of cookies for all the guests.

Everyone is invited!

Day 76: The other day, when my husband was in pre-op, they put a paper hospital gown on him. It was a new, special type of gown. A hose was hooked up to a port in the side of it, and hot air was pumped into it, warming him up. There was even a dial, so he could control the temperature setting. I wanted one of these and asked politely if I could have one, telling staff I was feeling chilly. They thought I was joking around, just suggesting it so it would put a smile on everyone's face. When I got to the level of bribing them and they realized I really was trying to get an electric heated robe from them, someone suggested that security should be called.

I thought about what my odds would be that the officer who had helped me find my van and my mind a few weeks ago would be the same cop responding to this call of "woman in pre-op harassing staff over articles of clothing." I wondered if it would be the same officer, if he would immediately hand cuff me, recognizing how menacing I am to the public safety, or if upon seeing my face once again, would take pity on me and merely whisper to staff, "I know this one, she's not quite right, but seems to be harmless." I decided to not take my chances and backed off on the hot blanket request.

But it got me thinking; I know it's too late for this holiday season, but wouldn't it be great if robes had a battery powered heating system? Perhaps I could patent this idea and market it for next year? Right then, my robe was lying on our bed and was being heated by one of the cats and the dog sleeping on top of it. This heating system only works if you're sleeping under it prior to Catzilla and Dog Gone jumping up on you. Not very portable.

My other great invention idea, was a razor with a three-foot handle so we women wouldn't have to behave like a gymnast or contortionist in the shower when shaving our legs every day. It could have a small mirror on it, for those 4" hairs that go untouched for sixteen years on the back of your ankles. The ones you don't know about until the day you're having lunch in a sunny cafe and your friend points it out in a really loud voice, leaving you conflicted, unsure if you should pluck the hair off your leg or stab her with a fork first.

How about a reclining chair, shaped like your mom's body, with seat heaters, so it feels like your mom was holding you again? It could even have speakers in the head rest and you could tape your mom's voice, saying comforting things to you. This would definitely be a vast improvement over the chair currently in our family room with the blown spring that motivates your bowels after only fifteen minutes of sitting there, no matter what you've had to eat. True, it's good for those days when you're a little constipated, but whoa, hold the door and don't sit down in that chair on those days when you've already beaten a path in the hallway carpet from the living room to the bathroom and it's only 9:21 a.m. Best to just stand behind that chair and let someone else take their chances with it.

Maybe when I get home I'll contact the "As Seen on TV" company and discuss these ideas for next year's holiday season. Or maybe, I'll just grab a glass of wine and a package of cookies, sit in the blown-spring chair, wrap up in my cat fur robe, and relax. That is, until the taped voice of my mom, in my head, yells at me to come empty the dishwasher.

Now that we're cancer free, I have more time to invent things I guess. Life is good!

Day 77: Navigating cancer would be easier if there was a user's manual with a trouble shooting guide in the back. Something staff could place in your hands, after your mind shuts down from the news that your loved one has cancer. Later, when your mind has cleared, or more likely, when it's gotten even foggier, you would remember that you have it, and refer to it.

Like last night. It would have been a good night for the user's manual. The surgical drain tube in my husband's leg had become disconnected in the morning and since there was no manual to refer to, we did what we thought was best; stuffed the tube back into the reservoir.

Oops.

I'm not sure why it didn't register in my mind that once the blood in the tube was exposed to air, it would coagulate plugging the tube, but somehow I forgot this most important fact.

By evening, as my exhaustion was wearing long, food had been forgotten for most of the day, and I was yearning for the Garfield the Cat pajamas even though happy hour hadn't even started yet, I looked at the drain tube and reservoir again.

Not good.

This was the moment when all that information that I said I would never use in college, suddenly came crashing back like waves on the back of my brain, sluicing down with just the facts ma'am. Words like sepsis, stroke, blood clots all started crowding my brain, screaming for attention.

I told my husband he needed to go to the ER.

"Nope, not gonna do it," was his adamant reply.

I told him we needed to call the doctor.

"Nope, not gonna do it."

I understood his reaction, as we're all sick and tired of doctors and hospitals, but I didn't agree with it. For some reason though, my exhaustion in combination with my gnawing hunger from not having eaten that day made me relent. I ordered a pizza instead. It was all I could handle doing. It was all my tired, weary brain could think to do as a secondary option if the doctor wasn't going to be called.

Had there been a trouble shooting guide to cancer, I could have looked up the code: "when the drain tube plugs and your husband refuses to go to the hospital" and I would not have found order a pizza as the answer. I guarantee it. But that's what I did.

When I got to the pizza place to pick up the pie, the owner was at the front counter. Probably a good thing too. She asked how things were going and I promptly burst into tears. I told her I was having a bad day and was sick and tired of hospitals. Sick and tired of cancer. She was her amazing self as always, comforting me, and sending me home, not only with a pizza, but with tissues too.

We ate dinner and somehow the pepperoni, mushrooms and onions provided a clarity of vision that I had been lacking. I called the surgeon. I called the oncologist. And the night fell into place. The plugged drain tube was removed by the surgeon in an emergency visit, the crisis passed and all was quiet at home once we returned again.

I am thinking about writing a trouble shooting guide to cancer though, so that others will have a reference and won't be lost. I know what the first code will be: "what to do when the doctor tells you that your loved one is in remission."

Call the local pizza joint, order 30 pies, and throw a really massive party. No tissues necessary.

Week 12: The New Normal

Day 78: Catzilla is currently on my desk, shredding the discharge papers from Tuesday's surgery. I know I should be angry, probably should take them away from her, but part of me feels like shredding them too, so I'm leaving her alone in her destruction.

It's as if, by shredding them, we're purging that part of our past, way back when, six days ago, when we were not cancer free. Now, with important past documents shredded, we can move forward.

Catzilla was one of the "hard to place" cats at the shelter, having lived the first eight months of her life in a cage. When I took my son over there to find a cat, we narrowed it down to three, and when the volunteer removed her from the cage, placed her in my son's arms and said, "You are the first people to look at her for over five months," I knew we had found our kitty.

She isn't an easy cat. She's not normal. How could she be, given the sad and remote first months of her life? Maybe, that's what called out to me most; life is hard, and if we give up on others just because it's hard, then what's the point? It's when we stick with it, dig down deep into our reserves and keep plodding along that makes it all worthwhile.

Catzilla isn't a lap kitty. Really doesn't like to be picked up or held. Minimal human contact is how she spends most of her days. But, when my husband was at his most sick with the chemotherapy, I would find her in his lap, purring, sleeping, pretending to be a normal cat for his sake. She knew he was sick, so she did what she could to make him feel better. The fact that he's NOT a cat person, adds a humorous touch to the whole thing, but Catzilla has endeared herself to him. He's still a dog person, but he's become a cat's-are-okay-sometimes person.

As I write this, she's moved on to the art room now, leaving a path of shredded documents and destruction in her wake. She's currently eating thread from the spool attached to my sewing machine. She'll either get all 500 yards down, or I'll have to reel it back out, like a fisherman retrieving a lost lure. I know, not normal.

Catitude isn't a normal cat either. My daughter found her, wounded, sick, emaciated, starving and weak, stumbling around in a state park, five hours from our home. When she walked through the door with this whisper-thin kitty, with its head split open with infection, stinking to high heaven, my first thought was, "It's too late. We have found this one too late." An hour later at the all-night veterinarian clinic, the doctor delivered confirmation to us that indeed, at 4 pounds, this full-grown cat, not a kitten like we had thought, was not going to make it through the night. Ever the fighter, especially when someone tells me it can't be done, I grabbed her back from the doctor and told him that I would let the cat die in my arms in my home with as much dignity as I could give her. Two sleepless nights later, she turned a corner, fought her way back from the edge of death and joined our family of misfits.

Weighing in at a whopping 7 pounds, this little cat makes up for her diminutive size by possessing the biggest, most loving heart of any animal I have ever known. Unfortunately, she still loves the hunt from her days in the state forest, so the downside of Catitude are the creatures, both great and small, that she drags home after an exhilarating day of hunting in our neighborhood.

It's okay that our pets are quirky and have sides to them that are difficult. People are the same way, have the same quirks sometimes. What's important, is that our cats and dog provide companionship, love, commitment, entertainment; but mostly they remind us that life can be hard, we just have to stick together. If we do that, whether we are two footed or four footed, another day will dawn with better opportunities and with brighter sunshine, illuminating all the important tax papers on my desk that the cat has shredded.

Day 79: I finally got my hair colored yesterday. For men, their response is, "What's the big deal?" For women, you're all out there exhaling, saying, "PHEW, that skunk stripe had to go!"

Bottom line is, the big deal about the hair color was that normal, everyday things had to be suspended. For seventy-eight days to be exact. I haven't been going to the chiropractor weekly. My dental appointment had to be rescheduled three times. I still hadn't seen the endocrinologist, despite making an appointment twice.

For me, getting to sit for an hour in the chair at the hair salon hour was relaxing. Touching base with my friend who has cut my hair for twenty-five years now was like a well anticipated homecoming. We have a shared history. Babies have been born, grown up, left for school. Hearts have been broken, mended and broken again. We talk about everything, everyone. It was a moment from "old normal", which I missed.

"New normal" is what your life becomes after cancer pulls up in your driveway. Sure, we're getting closer to "old normal" each day, obviously since I was able to get my hair colored. But the truth is, we will never again be back to the old "old normal". We can't, because once you have cancer move in, despite living in the town of remission, you're still a cancer survivor and all that goes along with that. This is our "new normal."

Time will pass, and this "new normal" will become what we're comfortable with, what we expect from life. We will go to barbeques in the summer, rake leaves in the fall, shovel mountains of snow in the winter, and haul arm loads of blooming daffodils into our home every spring when they emerge from under the melting snow. Time will pass, seasons will change, and all of us will grow older.

The only difference is that this time, living in the "new normal," with the passage of time and seasons, they will not only be marked by the ever-changing colors of nature all around us, but by the quarterly cat scans, MRI's and blood work that my husband will be subjected to, in order to ensure that cancer hasn't come back into our home and taken possession of our lives once again.

Day 80: It whispers around the corner as I enter the bedroom. It's sibilant voice, too low for me to make out its words. A quiet nagging, like a cold hand on the back of my neck. It beckons.

I glance in the corners, looking for it.

Is it there, near the IV pole, a bag of saline hanging idly waiting for the next chemo round?

There on the nightstand next to my husband's side of the bed? Stacked with tissue boxes, four remote controls, two pairs of broken glasses, some dusty pictures of the children, and a package of half eaten crackers?

Here, in the bathroom, amid medicinal lotions, creams, and wipes?

Behind a stack of towels, resting on the floor next to the toilet, placed there for those moments when the vomiting is so bad my husband cannot rise from the floor and must clean himself up there instead?

I sense its presence, hearing it call to me and now it's smell creeps into my nose, clogging my throat, filling my mind up with its grayness. I spin to leave the room, unsure of what direction it is coming at me. A strange mixture of alcohol, vomit, sadness, and fear, it fills me up, yet leaves me strangely empty.

Down two flights of stairs and into the kitchen, surely it hasn't followed me here.

Somehow though, it's moved faster than I, and it waits there, crouched on the counter like a decrepit old cat. I swipe at it, wishing it to be gone. Pain killers, vitamins, and anti-nausea pills go flying, but still it sits there, patiently waiting for my acceptance. It drapes itself heavy across my shoulders, and I am horrified to realize it fits me like a well-worn, much loved shawl; comforting, consoling, yet compressing, smothering and unyielding.

I stagger under its weight, unable to move. I take one last look around. It is all around me, having filled the spaces of my home, taken up residence here. Like a coat of paint in a color too harsh for human eyes, it colors all that our lives have become.

We may be cancer free, but now we are survivors of cancer, and we will be forever more. The memories of it live with us, here in our home.

It is everywhere.

Day 81: That we will face this Christmas season with the unwanted house guest cancer is somewhat disappointing, but given where we were three months ago, I can't complain.

I'm thinking about rolling the IV pole over next to the Christmas tree. Maybe even wrapping it with sparkly, gold garland. The vomit bucket will sit next to the gaily wrapped packages, assuming I make it to the mall and actually do some shopping in the next few days, then gaily wrap them. Saline filled syringes will find a home next to a candy filled bowl decorated with snowmen.

My husband will continue to sit in the living room under a heap of blankets, vacillating between freezing and sweating after the chemotherapy begins again. Maybe I'll buy a bunch of white blankets and he can be decorated as a living snowman, periodically waking up and announcing "Happy Birthday!" like Frosty does each year on the television. Then again, maybe I won't buy the white blankets as we have a black cat, brown cat and a spotted dog. Within a day, my husband would look like a semi-melted snowman that had been pelted by hair-ball spitting rabid racoons.

Yes, this Christmas will be a "new normal" Christmas, definitely not an "old normal" one. There will be joy, happiness, laughter, faith, grace, love and peace. But there will also be a strange compromise of "old normal" mixed with chemotherapy, pain, vomit, heartache, depression, sadness, and cancer too.

It's the script that we have been given, the one we are forced to act out right now. We need to make it work.

Nobody said we had to embrace it forever.

Day 82: We finally got the pathology report yesterday from the surgery. The tumor was 95% dead, which is what they were hoping for (YEAH!), all the margins were clean (DOUBLE YEAH!), and chemo resumes on December 11th (UN-YEAH).

I know, it seems a little silly to make my husband go through the hell of chemo three more times, despite being cancer free. It's just that, there's always that possibility of one rogue cancer cell. Camped out in some remote site in his body, resting up for the big day, when it decides to invite friends over and construct a tent in the shape of a tumor.

Dumping toxic, poisonous chemotherapy drugs into the bloodstream is the only thing that can find that one cancer cell and squash it.

There is one good thing about chemotherapy being on the 11th though. This is after the local church's Live Nativity, so we are holding our Hot Cider Night at our home and inviting everyone to stop in for a hot, steaming mug and then walk with us to the church to experience this beautiful recreation of the Birth of Christ. This yearly routine to our holidays will be deeply appreciated, as it is closer to old normal, than new normal and will provide us with a beautiful start to the holiday season.

Luckily the road is finished too, as walking to the church in quick-sand like gravel and mud would be an adventure that we're not willing to take, especially now that my husband has had one-third of his thigh removed. Pretty certain that Mary and Joseph probably didn't have a smoothly paved road leading to the creche. On the other hand, I doubt they had a llama, turkey or three-legged goat, which is what our town comes up with each year as "livestock." I've thought about offering to bring Catitude, figuring we could put a clever little hat and coat on her and transform her into a baby lamb. Then I remember her propensity for hunting and figure she would first take down the turkey, then go after the llama.

At least this year, our sons are old enough that they won't stick their mittens into the space heaters placed strategically around the hay bales we sit on. Nothing says "Merry Christmas" like the smell of burning, wet wool, and nothing stops the angels from singing, faster than a shrieked, "That boys mitten is on fire and his hand is still in it."

Maybe the "new normal" isn't so bad after all.

Day 83: I called my son's pediatrician's office today. The receptionist who knows me answered. When I identified myself, she quickly replied, "You sound better."

Huh? "Compared to when?" I asked her.

She sputtered, "Don't get me wrong, but back in September when I spoke to you last, you were woman on the edge."

I was immediately reminded of the phone conversation she was referring to and she was right, I sounded better today.

The thing is, back in September, I really thought I was handling all of this well. Keeping all the spinning plates spinning. Now, looking back through the eyes of this woman, I realized, I was just barely hanging on back then. I really was woman on the edge. I just didn't know it. Thankfully I didn't know it, because I just might have paused long enough, to let a plate, or two, or all of them drop.

Now the worst is past. The plates are spinning, most of them on their own again, with little or no help from me.

I'm probably still woman on the edge, but today, it's because I'm just a mom of teenagers, with a dog who thinks she's a mountain goat, and one cat that thinks she's a dog, another cat that we think is an alien, and the holidays are approaching.

This is a good edge to be on right now.

Day 84: Make a list and check it twice. Christmas is right around the corner and this seemed like a good idea when I woke up this morning. A checklist would help me assess what I have accomplished toward getting ready for the holidays and what still needed to be finished.

Checklist:

Three Christmas trees with all the lights burnt out on them. Check.

Payment to the Post Office for the PO Box, unpaid, now shredded by the cat. Check.

Forgotten Amaryllis bulb found growing in a box in the dining room, misshapen and mutant. Check.

Lights on the mantle keep falling off, making loud crashing noises. Check.

Freezer making noises as if on the verge of immediate collapse. Totally full. Check.

Catzilla keeps shredding wrapping paper from the few purchased and wrapped presents currently under the tree. Check.

Catitude keeps climbing up onto the live, fully decorated tree in the family room, knocking it over. One whole side of the tree is now misshapen and is missing ornaments as they have all broken. Check.

Washing machine refusing to properly execute the spin cycle for three loads. Check.

All this before 8 a.m. Check.

Just another day in paradise.

Cancer free paradise, that is.

Day 85: When we moved here years ago, we had an artificial tree we brought with us and for Christmas we would set it up in our living room. We had no decorations, no money to buy any, and resale shops were not the rage that they are today. What to do?

It was a beautiful tree and seemed a shame not to use it, so I had my kids make ornaments. I had playdates with other moms, and their kids made ornaments for the tree too.

Time has passed, but each year, I put this tree up, using only the ornaments that were handmade by family and friends. Of all the decorations that I have in my home, this living tribute to my children's younger years is my most cherished of decorations.

There's the drinkable yogurt containers that we turned into snowmen. My youngest was four years old that year, and when we had a dozen of these made, he looked at them and said, "It would be cool if dad drilled holes in the back so we could put the lights inside of them." After the momentary stunned silence that only something that profound coming from a preschooler could have on us, my husband whipped out the drill, and we had ourselves some amazing lights.

There's the gingerbread people cut from neon

colored card stock, decorated with pom poms, noodles, and string. My daughter's friends helped with these, and much to their horror, fifteen years later, these crazy, paper people still dance around the tree, making us laugh at them each year.

There's the cyclops Santa, cyclops Snowman and cyclops Spider, keeping a watchful eye on the cat who claims this tree as her personal fort. They started out with two eyes, but somewhere over time, they've been reduced to uni-eyed ornaments, odd in their appearance, but loved all the same.

There's the angel on top of the tree, constructed from a paper plate, a drinking straw and some staples. Her claim to fame has never been that she is beautiful, but rather that she is hard working, sturdy, and dependable, shining her straw star down on the tree and all those who dwell there for the entire Christmas season.

There's garland made from colored pasta that can't be hung too low on the tree as various animals in our home like to snack on them. There's also two ice cream cones, real, food-stuff legitimate ice cream cones, that some over-ambitious second grade teacher had my older two kids paint with polyurethane when they were in her class. Each year as I pull them from the box, I again wonder at what this woman was thinking putting paint brushes into the hands of seven- year-olds and telling them to dip that into nasty chemicals. The dog doesn't seem to mind the chemicals though, so these also must be hung high upon the tree.

I know it's probably silly that I put this tree up each year. I know it's also seen as some gaudy, tragic, pathetic misrepresentation of Christmas to others. But I love each ornament. I love the creativity and joy that went into making all of them. This is what the holiday is about for me.

Homemade, from the heart.

Family. Friends. Togetherness.

Love. Faith. Hope. Peace. Joy.

I'm just glad we will all be together this holiday season and that my husband is now considered, cancer-free.

Week 13: Ninety Days in Hell; I Think I'll Have More Egg Nog

Days 86: The nutrition label on the eggnog bottle should include the following: Not to be taken while in a Chemo Fog. Should you accidentally ingest eggnog while stoned on Chemo Fog, seek assistance from a close personal friend who can guide you back to an outfit that matches and is not stained, help you remember to run carpool and provide you with a dinner that does not require the use of flames for reheating, as fire should be avoided at all costs. Candy canes should also be avoided as the wrappers are too difficult to remove while floating in an eggnog laced Chemo Fog.

Day 87: You ever wondered about those women who are featured in the pages of "Home Spectacular" magazine? You know the ones, they are sitting in their perfectly pressed cream, linen slacks, with a silk blouse that costs more than my entire years clothing budget at the Resale-o-Rama, on a white couch that screams "the photo's you are about to see of children and a dog are all fake because my white couch is impossibly clean."

There is always some clever article to go along with the stark, crisp photographs, indicating that "Mirabella" is a corporate lawyer, wife to "Trey Louis Turner IV" a neurosurgeon specializing in microsurgery of the blasto-histo-what-not in the brain, and they live in this amazing home with their two children, "Bella Tery" and "Mira Lou" and their dog, Bennett.

The article always raves about how perfect their lives are and how happy they all are, every single day. The pictures show sparkling white rooms with just the right amount of muted colored accent pillows. Nothing bad has ever happened, nor will it ever in this home. Bad things can't happen to these people, their couch might get dirty.

When I was younger, I used to dream about living in these homes. I would hold the magazine up close to my face, concentrate on every detail of their home. I would close my eyes, shutting out the chaos and disorder that was my home, and picture myself there instead. That I had dirty feet and hands while I was doing it, never registered in my dream world. Surely, if I was transported to this fairy-tale world, some far-away forgotten fairy godmother who would take me there would make sure I was cleaned up first before plopping me down on that glorious couch. That I was usually sitting on our ugly, brown-plaid couch, encapsulated in protective, plastic covers, would be forgotten until the moment I would go to stand up and because we lacked air conditioning, my skin would peel away from the plastic like skin off a peach.

My dreams and fantasies of these homes and these women lasted until my teen years, when I finally realized, they were probably, at least to some extent, fake.

By then I had learned that life is messy. Blood, vomit, tears, dirt, spills, chaos; eventually all things are going to get stained, used, abused and destroyed. By then, I had also learned that living a comfortable life (we had finally convinced our parents to remove the plastic coverings from the couch, but we still didn't have air conditioning) was more important than having beautiful possessions.

I'll admit, a new couch for Christmas would be lovely. The one we have now has been used as a cat scratching post for too many years. The weird stain on the left seat cushion is from my accidentally grabbing the kitchen cleaner spray containing bleach instead of the Febreze when unexpected guests showed up three years ago. There's only so much wear and tear you can hide with throw pillows and an ancient afghan blanket from someone's great aunt. If we tried to donate this lovely gem to Resale-o-Rama, they would laugh us out of their parking lot.

But everyone is healthy right now, jammed onto the couch, eating popcorn, watching Christmas movies together and that is the best Christmas gift anyone could ask for.

Day 88: This morning in the shower, I went to hang my towel up after I was finished and realized my husband's towel wasn't there. I thought back to that day, months ago, when I was freaking out about the possibility of him not making it and me finding myself possibly alone.

Who would dig the hair out of the bath tub drain?

Who would show the boys how to shave?

Who would I share a giant pretzel with at baseball games?

Who would help line up my putt shots on the greens?

Who would I spend the rest of my life with?

I know the answer now to those questions and all the others pertaining to us as a couple.

My husband will take care of all those quirky little problems that I either cannot or will not do. All of those messy situations in life, when dad is needed, and not mom.

All of those times when, despite all the feminism progress we all have worked so hard for is set aside, because it's just easier to hand the guy standing next to you the pickle jar and say, "Can you please open this for me?"

There was a certain level of fear of the future a few months ago, but it's gone now. It was erased, the day the oncologist said, "you should consider yourself cancer free now."

Day 89: This is probably going to sound weird, but I'm having a moment because it's Day 89. That means, tomorrow will be Day 90, and for some reason, being in the 90's and still dealing with a little cancer in our lives, seems to be too long for me.

When I think about friends and family who dealt with cancer for years after diagnosis, it should seem like ninety days isn't much.

Maybe it's having to go through the holidays with chemotherapy wedged in the middle of the month. Traditions are being side-lined, parties missed, decorations despite being started at the beginning of November, have taken until this morning to finally be put into place.

Maybe it's the knowledge, that after the 90's, we enter the triple digit days, and ironically, Day 100 will be the start of chemo round 4, which is a mere 11 days away.

Maybe it's because one of my friend's last wishes years ago, was to have her Christmas tree decorated, and shortly after the last ornament was put in place, she quietly let go of the epic battle she had waged with cancer. Today, as I sat looking at our tree, I thought of her.

Maybe that's what's been niggling at the back of my brain all morning. Thinking of her and remembering, not that last moment, for I wasn't there and only heard the story afterwards, but what happened between the two of us, four months before she passed away.

We were on the beach on vacation together, the children building sand castles, swimming and shouting. I turned to her and said, "We have to do this again next summer. It's so relaxing for us and fun for the kids."

There were no tears in her eyes, no trembling lips, just a resolute look on her face, as she replied, "I won't be here."

My mouth opened, shut, opened, shut, words escaping me, finding no voice. She saw my discomfort and replied, "It's okay. I've accomplished everything I was meant to do. It's going to be fine. You'll see."

There's the message really. If our lives were to end tomorrow, would we leave unfinished business behind, or would we be at peace with all that we have accomplished, having squeezed every precious minute, out of every precious day?

Could you say; "It's okay. I've accomplished everything I was meant to do. It's going to be fine. You'll see."

Day 90: I've been wracking my brains about Christmas gifts for everyone. I usually start in September or October, squirreling away trinkets, baubles and even a ten-speed bike one year. For someone who is not good at keeping secrets, hiding the gifts for entire months takes every ounce of reserves I have.

But here it is, less than a week away from Christmas and no gifts have been bought. Nothing. Not even a small bag of chocolates that could be sub-divided among us on Christmas morning as some small nod toward the holidays.

True, shopping the past few months has been an adventure. Each trip has involved a quick run into the store, grab anything that is remotely nutritional, and dart toward the check-out line before the next carpool jaunt to pick up my son's or husband.

On the "good" shopping days, I make it out of the store without running into anyone and make it home with some sort of vegetable, a passable fruit and enough milk to last a few days. On the "bad" shopping days, I run into someone who asks how we are all doing, which always results in my bursting into tears, while trying to convince them that we are all "just fine." On these days, time is consumed by the emotional outburst and not by actual, active shopping, so we land up eating whatever I can grab off the end-caps at the register. That our local grocery store tends to stock only cookies, juice boxes and video tapes on these end-caps is the excuse I use on the nights we dine on dinner expressly made for us by those dependable, tree-dwelling elves.

But, this is merely an excuse. During all those sleepless nights, I could have ordered gifts on-line and had them delivered to our home. I could have paid extra to have them gift wrapped, saving me from that most hated task.

The truth though, is that when cancer enters your home, like all other major illnesses, it brings your perspective back in focus. You finally look at everything around you with clear vision, you hear with open ears and open hearts.

You finally understand that there is no greater gift than good health, family and friends. That these are life's most precious gifts and nothing else compares.

Merry Cancer-free Christmas to Us.

Day 91: I woke feeling terribly guilty about not having presents for the kids under the tree this year, despite my deep, philosophical thoughts from yesterday. After talking with my husband, he called some of his friends and asked if they would come over to watch some football games (and him) while I hit the mall.

Despite being born a female, I'm just not one of those women who was born to shop. I avoid the mall at all costs, preferring resale shops, musty, old antique shops and the occasional jaunt to a strip mall. But the big mall, with all the people, noise, crowds and confusion, not my cup of tea.

But guilt over the kids Christmas was driving me and the thought of a few hours by myself while my husband was being taken care of sealed the deal.

With no lists from anyone (bad idea), no sizes or dimensions (worse idea), relatively little sleep (turn back now!), and only one cup of coffee in my system (have you lost your mind?!?), I set off for the mall.

Christmas is in a few days. I thought everyone would be done with their shopping. They would all be tucked cozily up under blankets, next to a fire, sipping hot chocolate, while watching holiday movies that remind us all to be decent human beings. They don't have loved ones with cancer, so they have had months to get all their shopping done.

Wrong.

Traffic was a crazy, log-jam of cars at every intersection. By the time I had made my way to the entrance to the mall parking lot I thought I was home free. It hadn't registered in my mind that all these people going to the mall, would be parking their cars at the mall.

I stalked shoppers leaving the mall for over twenty minutes until someone led me to their parked car and gave me their spot. By then, almost an entire precious hour of my time had been used up and I felt discouraged, angry and defeated. A seven-mile drive had consumed one-third of my shopping time.

If the parking lot was a nightmare, the mall was a horror story of epic proportions. Hundreds, possibly thousands of shoppers, crammed into stores, waiting in lines, clogging the escalators. There was no escaping the throngs of people clamoring for those last-minute purchases that were necessary to make their Christmas celebration complete.

Plunging into the masses, I immediately found myself standing in line at a store I wasn't familiar with. Somehow, I had been re-routed from my bee-line toward the clothing store that I knew my daughter liked, into this strange shop where everyone was pawing through bins filled with distressed looking shoes. When I asked the woman next to me what the fuss was about, she looked at me like I was from some distant planet and said, "This is the latest shipment from that cool, new designer who all the kids are following right now! Here, I'll help you find your kids sizes."

I mumbled what I thought would fit my daughter and within minutes Most Helpful Woman Ever had thrust an old, semi-moist sponge into my hands. Quickly I dropped it back into the bin with a loud, "Yuck!" and turned to chastise her for giving me someone else's garbage from the bin. Without knowing it, when I had uttered this one word amongst this crowd, I had cast myself as the fashion train-wreck that I have always been.

"What did you say?" she quietly whispered, as if the famous cool, new designer might be close at hand and could hear our exchange and become enraged. That the crowd of people around us was quiet I suppose should have been expected. What I had not expected, was that the entire store was quiet as a church on Sunday. All eyes and ears were on me, the traitorous fashion failure, who had offended everyone when I dropped the alien foam pads back in the bin.

"Um, I said yuck. You handed me someone's old kitchen sponge. I don't know why it is in there, but it was," I said, desperately searching the crowd for an ally.

"It's actually an amazing pair of shoes made from an exotic mushroom found only in the deserts. They pay fair wages to the local inhabitants to find and harvest the mushrooms. By purchasing the shoes, you are helping to save the desert from distinction," she fumed, pointing at the entire bin of fungus shaped roughly in the shapes of shoes.

"Extinction, not distinction," I responded, "and I'm not sure the desert could ever become extinct and what kind of mushrooms grow in the desert? It's pretty dry there. Are you sure these are not from some local guy trying to have one over on you?"

"I feel nothing but pity for your poor children. You should be worried that they will be laughed at in January when they get to school and they are wearing the wrong shoes," replied Most Hurtful Woman Ever. Then she turned her back on me and started muttering under her breath to the others around her about the faded magenta jeans I was wearing that went out of style thirty years ago.

I'm back home now. No fungus flip-flops under the tree. Just a few packages containing socks, ugly sweaters, gift cards and a little candy. The ugly sweaters I got at the Goodwill store on my way home. Someone else's cast-offs that were still in like-new condition. My kids won't care, they know that I predominantly shop at resale stores. They're use to this. The candy was some grab-n-go from the front register area at the local convenience mart.

I'm hoping no one makes the "well, it's the thought that counts" comment on Christmas morning, because I most likely will burst into tears about this half-hearted attempt at Christmas gifts. There wasn't even much thought put into them except, "I have no time, no energy, no anything left inside of me, except exhaustion, so this is my best," kind of thought.

My guilt over the kids' Christmas is still there, but now it's a low-level guilt that is only slightly coloring the upcoming holiday. I think it's due to the one thing that I cannot fix, the one gift that I cannot wrap up and put under the tree. I would if I could, but I can't.

I can't give them a 100% healthy father for Christmas this year. We still have one more round of chemotherapy to get through, so we're not there yet. With no hair, translucent, papery-thin skin, angry boils erupting daily on his head and neck, my husband still looks quite sick. His energy level is so low, consumption of just a meal exhausts him. Part of me understands that Christmas Day will be celebrated in small packets of time, wedged in between naps that my husband will require just to get through the day. I also need to remember the message of the season, which came to me while shopping for the ugly sweaters.

Peace on Earth, Goodwill Toward Men.

Week 14: Inhale

Day 92:

Crash.

Burn.

Explode.

Sink.

Swim.

Survive.

Breathe.

Inhale.

No one should have to go through chemotherapy during the holidays.

No one should have to deal with cancer during the holidays.

No one should have to deal with cancer. EVER.

Exhale.

Breathe.

Day 93: We're in those pre-chemotherapy, anxiety filled days. Where sleep eludes us, despite a to-the bone-weariness and a deep down in the soul exhaustion draped on our shoulders like an old blanket. My face has that heavy, saggy, not-quite-right feel to it which comes with a lack of sleep and a weekend of bad food choices.

While I dread the upcoming days because I remember what each and every minute will hold for us, my husband dreads the chemotherapy but with a total lack of memory. His conscious mind shoved the horror filled memories of the chemical dragon breathing fire through his blood stream into the back corners of his mind. Covering it with a musty tarp made from the sweeter memories of days at college, the craziness of the holidays and his beloved fantasy football team.

This mixture of dread and exhaustion slows down the days, warping time, expanding each minute, until they are infinitely long. The focus is now making it to 3:30 p.m. on Friday, when the last drop will rage through his bloodstream, and like weary warriors, we will battle through rush hour traffic to arrive victorious at our home.

True, my husband is cancer free, but this chemotherapy is like an insurance premium. You hate to make the payment, but you fear the consequences of not doing so.

In two days, we will walk a long distance on this journey without end. Today, we're just going to drink tea, nap, and ready ourselves. Sit by the fire, playing games with the kids, go to bed early as it's Christmas Eve.

Sometimes that's the best part of this walk in grace, the quiet moments spent with family and friends. The celebration of laughter, kindness, joy, peace and love. The gentle steps taken from the kitchen sink where the tea cup rests, to the bed, where the hand knitted quilt quietly calls to us.

Day 94: Merry Christmas!!!

I always marvel at the fact that during the entire year, my children are incapable of getting out of bed without two alarm clocks going off on either sides of their beds, dynamite lit under them and a ton of cajoling. But come Christmas morning, 3:38 a.m. sees them chattering loudly in our family room, stuffing their faces with chocolate and arguing over who is going to be saddled with the onerous task of waking the parents up, despite our already being awake due to the noise.

That they are now teenagers, creatures who typically sleep up to 14 straight hours when there are tasks such as seal coating the drive-way to be done, makes me wonder how they could possibly function this early in the morning. But here it is, Christmas morning and the noise coming from the family room indicates that everyone, including the animals, is there, awaiting the arrival of the parents.

Which is taking some time, because we have a little cancer in the home and it makes life move at a funny pace.

My husband is awake, but feeling so fatigued, that even the thought of just sitting up is too much at this moment. In an attempt to balance my husband's need with more rest, with my children's enthusiasm for unwrapping gifts, I have brought a cup of coffee up to the bedroom for him with a plea that he just get up for one hour.

The other struggle I have right now, is that the guilt about the presents now that the moment is upon us, is super heavy again on my shoulders. What was I thinking buying used clothing for the kids for their Christmas gifts? True, most of our savings account has been emptied this year on medical bills, parking fees, tolls, gasoline, medical supplies, and a litany of OTC's that haven't done any good, for anyone. Still, could I not have come up with something better for these three precious gifts that have dealt with a sick dad these past months?

Precious gifts.

Oh, how could I have forgotten? Especially on this morning, of all mornings? These three precious gifts that came into our lives years ago. They bring us joy, happiness, tears, laughter, smiles, frustrations, and love.

They have dealt with a sick father, but like all children, they are resilient, full of hope and optimism for the future. They have weathered the past few months and will be fine during the upcoming weeks. They will accept whatever is in those wrapped presents, because the one present they wanted most isn't wrapped up under the tree.

The one present they have wanted more than anything this year, is hobbling slowly down the hallway in a faded robe toward the chaos and noise, cup of coffee in his hand, a huge, smile on his face.

What a precious gift life is.

Day 95: The most powerful computer in the world is the human brain. Capable of processing millions of bits of information, it also has the capacity to distort our perceptions, create something that isn't there, and make us believe it.

This happened today for my husband. By early afternoon, he wasn't feeling well. When I returned home from running errands at dinnertime, he told me he had the stomach flu. He said he was really sick. His super computer brain had made him believe he was sick, even creating real, physical symptoms. He said he had the stomach flu so bad, that he would have to reschedule the chemotherapy that was supposed to start tomorrow morning.

Had he told me that he had the regular flu, or maybe even food poisoning, I might have actually paused to consider his symptoms. But he told me it was stomach flu, which I immediately diagnosed as: one brick too many in his overburdened backpack.

To be clear, there is no such thing as stomach flu. Influenza A & B, just doesn't go there. True, there's a virus called Gastroenteritis that loves the stomach, but it's not the flu. So, when he told me that it was the stomach flu, I jumped to the conclusion, that his subconscious mind was trying to give him an out from the upcoming treatment. I felt for him; no one looks forward to chemotherapy, and rounds three through five are the worst in terms of emotional and spiritual strength to get through.

But, I felt strongly that this was just an overburdened backpack filled with too many bricks and not a physical disease. My job was to take some bricks, put them in my backpack and carry them for a while. So I did.

The transfer was easy. Cup of tea, some homeopathic supplements, a warm blanket, a movie shared together on the couch, and his load was lightened enough to go on. His symptoms went away, and his super computer brain was able to refocus again on what needed focusing on: his fantasy football team.

No matter what our journey is each day, our burden to bear is always lightened by those who take the journey with us. Some days I'll carry extra bricks, some days you will need to carry them for me. This is how life goes on.

Day 96: Chemotherapy.

What can I say that hasn't been said already? It sucks, it's hard, it's evil, it's awful, it's a lot of terrible adjectives, the list just goes on and on and on.

This time though, there were some bright spots. It is the last round, so this is the last Day One Chemotherapy, hopefully forever. Also, I was able to stay the entire eight hours with my husband. With the kids on holiday breaks, no frantic rushing into the city, dropping my husband off, then rushing back out into the suburbs to get them to school. As an added bonus, about half the city seemed to have taken the week in between Christmas and New Year's Eve off, so traffic was super light.

I truly thought my husband and I would watch movies together, talk, laugh and the time would fly by, getting us one day closer to DONE.

Boy was I wrong. As soon as he was hooked up, he closed his eyes and within five minutes was gently snoring. Looking around the chemotherapy ward, I realized this was exactly how all the other patients were handling the toxic drips. I settled in with the book I had brought.

Time passed, days it felt like, although it was only three hours and finally my husband woke up. He said he felt hot, parched, nauseous, itchy, uncomfortable. The nurse came in, handed him a cup of ice water, dumped something into his PICC line, patted his hand and walked out of his pod. Five minutes later he complained that he was hungry, still thirsty, cold, sweaty, anxious, feverish and had a weird taste in his mouth. A second nurse arrived, shot more meds into the PICC line, handed him a second cup of ice water and a packet of crackers. She was wise enough not to pat his hand on her way out.

Whatever that medication was, it seemed to take the edge off, so he tried getting some of the lunch down that I had brought for him. Crackers, peanut butter on bread, applesauce, easy foods to both swallow and digest. As soon as half of the sandwich was down, he stated that he thought he was going to be sick. I went to the nursing station and quietly asked if there were stronger meds that he could be given, indicating that the first two drugs didn't seem to be working.

The three nurses at the station did one of those side long glances at each other, the kind that indicated that there was something uncomfortable that needed to be said and silently they were trying to decide who would be the bearer of the bad news. The senior nurse finally spoke up and in a hushed whisper told me that my husband had received the strongest medications possible and that he went through this "phase" each and every treatment cycle. As I wasn't sure what she meant by "phase," I asked her to clarify.

Apparently, my husband's super-computer brain was making him feel "sick" each chemotherapy cycle and because I had never been able to sit through an entire day with him, I had missed this "phase." They assured me that it was all psychological and it would pass soon, we all just needed to ignore it.

I walked back to my husband, who looked up at me with what looked like hope in his eyes. No matter if he was making himself feel sick or the chemotherapy drugs were making him nauseous, he definitely didn't feel well and I needed to do something. Sitting there, waiting for the next hand pat from staff wouldn't work for me.

"I'll be right back. I have to go get something for you down in the pharmacy," I told him.

He nodded, closed his eyes, laid his head back against the reclining chair and seemed to relax a bit. That he probably was thinking that I was going to get him stronger medications made me feel a bit terrible given what I was planning on purchasing. But I couldn't come up with any alternative, so I stuck to my plan.

The elevators were packed, so I opted for the stairs. Probably a good choice given how overweight I am, except that I got lost and somehow landed up outside of the maternity ward. I went back up one flight of stairs, but found myself in the pulmonology ward, despite my being convinced that I had only come down one flight of stairs in the first place. I spun to go back to the stairs again, but the sensible part of me, what small, sliver of it is left, told me to go to the elevators and wait with everyone else.

Once on the elevator, I realized the problem, when I noticed that the elevator doors opened on both ends, depending on whether you needed the old wing or the new wing of the hospital. With oncology in the new wing and the pharmacy in the old section, it was almost forty-five minutes before I was back up onto the cancer ward.

Of course, my husband was sleeping. Which was fine as I wasn't too sure what I had bought for him would make a difference anyway. I sat down, picked up my book and another three hours crawled by.

When he finally opened his eyes, and saw that there were still two hours to go, it was like a pin popping an air mattress. The air goes out, it just takes a little time. Slowly his arms and shoulders sagged, then his face drooped, then his whole body seemed to curl back into the chair. He saw me looking at him, plastering what felt like a fake, "hope you feel better soon!" smile on my face. He told me he felt like angry beess were swarming through his body, that his clothes were too tight, that his skin hurt, and that he still felt nauseous.

I smiled bigger then, putting my best, "I'm trying to win an Oscar for Leading Lady," smile on and told him I had gotten him something from the pharmacy that would help. He straightened up and held out his hand, clearly thinking it was meds.

Still smiling, I pulled a can of ginger ale and two Styrofoam cups from a brown paper bag. Opened the can of soda and poured it into a cup. I started pouring the ginger ale from one cup to the other, each time releasing the carbonation from the sugar sweet molecules. When there was no fizz left, I handed him the cup and told him to drink it up.

I could tell he was disappointed, but he was also thirsty and this was better than plain old ice water, so he took a sip.

Then another. And another.

And for the first time that day, he smiled. He held out his hand for mine and squeezed it tight. We sat there holding hands while he finished the flat ginger ale, smiling the whole time.

Laughter is always the best medicine, but when it is dark where you are standing and you can't find anything to laugh about, the second best medicine, might just be a can of de-fizzed ginger ale and someone to hold your hand.

Day 98: Today was a quiet day on the chemotherapy ward. My husband slept for almost the entire eight hours, providing me with ample time to let my thoughts wander back over this walk in grace that we have taken. The highs, the middles, the "who knew we could go this low," lows. Wandering back over the past three months, I started to tick off the days I really didn't think I could get through and decided to pat myself on the back for having survived them.

I realized as I was tripping down memory lane, that one of the hardest days for me, was not during the chemotherapy weeks, not during radiation treatments or even surgery. The hardest day for me, had actually been an almost nothing day.

Or it would have been a nothing day, but because we had nothing going on that day, my daughter asked us if we would re-create some of the treatment days so she could capture the images with her camera for an upcoming project at college.

Seemed like a simple request, one that we could easily comply with, so we agreed to walk through the past few months, re-staging scenes with IV poles, bandages, surgical masks, medicine bottles, and various medical supplies. Staging each photo, standing there waiting for the flash, it really was moments that were not filled with fear, trauma, pain or heartache. All I had to do, was merely stand where I was told to stand; do what I was told to do.

But something shifted deep, down inside me after the camera flash went off for the first time. It was if we had backed up time to the point where the PICC line was first being placed in my husband's arm, way back during the first week of treatment. Standing there, "faking" an IV push of heparin into a "fake" line in his arm, my hands started to tremor, my heart started to race. Anxiety welled up, filling my thoughts with one simple phrase: "NO."

I didn't say anything to my daughter or husband. Neither of them noticed either. I controlled my shaking hands best that I could, swallowed my anxiety and dread, and stumbled through each staged scene. Scenes of his medication bottles by the bedside. Scenes of face masks covering all but our eyes. Scenes flashing by, miniscule time capsules of the past few months. All of them, while my heart pounded, my hands shook and my stomach clenched.

By the time we got to the photo of me wrapping a clean bandage on his surgically altered leg, I was covered in a cold, clammy sweat. Part of my dread must have been coming through by this time, for my daughter kept chastising me to "stop making that face."

Looking back now, it seems all so silly to have reacted the way I did. I'm glad that I pushed myself to the end of the photo shoot too, for the last photograph of our two hands, clasped, wearing our wedding bands, is a beautiful testament, to our marriage and to standing by one another no matter what.

Week 15: Exhale

Day 99: As parents, we don't expect to outlive our children. It's not the natural order of life. Unfortunately though, sometimes a child is taken from us, and as parents we have to deal with this loss.

I witnessed this first hand with the loss of both my brother and brother-in-law at early ages. It was as if, when the child left this earth too early, the ripping of their soul from this world caused a huge tear in the souls of their mothers. A piece of each woman's soul, literally left this earth with the child when they left. They were never whole again. They couldn't be. Something fundamental had been taken from them, and no matter how much time passed, they couldn't quite heal.

How to go on with a piece of you missing?

I searched for the answer to this while watching my mother struggle after my brother was gone. She would spend long afternoons, staring out the window, searching for answers where none existed. Spend entire days laying in bed, incapable of rising, eating, or moving. Her soul was torn to shreds and no amount of time would mend it back to the whole that it once had been.

One day while I was at her bedside, I just started talking. Not knowing what to say, I still felt the need to fill the empty space with words, not silence.

"I don't know why, but you were chosen for this path. The only thing I can figure, is that you are stronger than the rest of us. Strong enough to bear this heavy burden and continue on the journey where others would be unable to tread. Strong enough to lift up your head, look life in its face and agree to face the day and the challenges in front of you. You were chosen for this path and as much as you don't want to walk it, how you walk it is an example to the rest of us, so you need to be the best example you can be. You need to show all of those around you, that bad things happen to good people, with no explanation or reason, and life still goes on. My brother may be gone, but there are still plenty of us that desperately need you, and we need you to be healthy and whole, walking this path with us. We still need you."

My mother was never whole again, the tear in her soul almost visible each and every day. But she eventually rejoined all of us on this walk in grace. She became a shining example of how, in the face of devastation and tragic loss, each day, we all still need to pick up our backpack filled with bricks and continue on the journey.

Day 100: LAST DAY OF CHEMOTHERAPY!!!! It's hard to believe that this glorious day is finally here, but it is!!!!!

Of course, once on the ward, my husband fell immediately asleep after the drip was started, so I was left with the same, boring book I have kept in my purse these last three days. I was too keyed up to sit still though. I kept popping up, walking around the hallways, chatting with whoever didn't have their eyes focused on their cell phones. Each time I passed my husband's chemotherapy pod, I would think, "Five more minutes finished!" then keep walking. Luckily for the staff I didn't announce the time as I would pass them, only nodding in their direction solemnly.

When I had logged about 57 laps, I started to drive myself crazy, which was 47 laps past when I had driven the receptionist crazy. With the sun shining outside and the fresh fallen snow from the day before, I decided to take a short jaunt outside in the hopes of burning off some of this pent-up energy.

I told the head nurse that I was going out into the courtyard for five minutes, to which she replied, "take your time," which really meant, "you are driving all of us completely crazy with your incessant pacing, please give us a break and don't come back for 30 minutes." I just grinned and nodded to her, then headed for the stairway.

And got lost, of course.

Old wing, new wing, maybe they lose patients in there, maybe they don't, but it's a crazy, rat-maze of hallways, stairwells, twists and turns. I asked three different people for directions to the outdoor courtyard, actually pointing through a third-floor window at one point that "down there, outside," was where I wanted to go. A kindly, elderly lady finally took hold of my arm and chatting all the way, got me to my destination.

When we finally reached the front entrance, with the courtyard beyond, I realized she didn't have a winter coat and pointed this out to her. She laughed, said she wasn't going outside, that she actually spends some of her day, helping lost people find their way in the hospital and she would be returning to one of the upper floors to look for the next lost soul. I laughed along with her, thanked her profusely, then told her to stop back in a half hour as I would need guidance to find my way back upstairs.

Then I turned to the front door and marched outside. The air was cold, bracing, slightly damp, indicating that more snow might be on its way. I didn't care, I turned left, striding down the courtyard. I hadn't known why I wanted to come down here so badly until I got to the front door. Then I realized why this was so important, especially on this day.

I walked over to the twisted sycamore tree with the park bench that was missing a back-slat and sat down.

This is where the journey started. This walk in grace. We had come here that first morning, met with all the doctors, then during a break in appointments, came out here to sit on this bench. We had eaten the lunch I had brought, having a life-long aversion to hospital food. Talk had been sparse, both of us processing what the morning had held, wondering what the afternoon would possess. The sun had been hot over-head and the leaves had provided some welcoming shade. Late summer was in high swing, beating the last drops of moisture out of the grass, flowers, plants and trees. So many people were out walking past us, oblivious to our pain, despair and worry. No one looked our way, no one stopped to offer condolences or assistance. We were solitary soldiers, an army of two, facing our worst opponent yet, cancer.

Now, months later, sitting there on that frost-rimed bench, the impossible cold slowly seeping into my joints, I realized, that despite the bone-deep chill, I felt exhilarated. I felt as if a sun possessing a trillion points of light was burning brightly within me, warming me. The few people who passed me by, heads lowered against the cold, were often startled at my manic greetings, called out to them from my perch on this bench. Grace, happiness, love, peace, warm feelings of gratitude, relief and joy, all spilled out of me, looking to others for a place to land.

I'm not sure how long I sat on that bench, under that gnarled, deformed sycamore tree. I might still be there, if not for my patron saint "grandma guide," wearing nothing but her hand-knitted sweater. She had come all the way out to the bench to get me. Kindly, she took my arm, raised me up and told me it was time to go back inside. We linked arms as we sauntered back toward the hospital, neither of us talking.

When we were back in the lobby, I turned to her and asked her how she had known where to find me.

The smile that lit her face was beautiful, filled with a special light of someone deeply touched by faith and grace. "They all find their way to the 'Survivors Tree,' on the last day of chemotherapy," she replied. "I knew when I found you in the hall with the early light of triumph in your eyes and heart, that you would make your way there." She hugged me, told me congratulations, then gently shoved me toward the chemotherapy ward.

We are at the base of the backside of the mountain now. We were resting in that sweet little stop-over town called Recovery for some time, holding our breath, waiting for the moment we were given clearance to start the journey toward Remission. When we were finally given small signs that we could take baby steps toward that beautiful destination, we still found ourselves holding our breath, unwilling to tempt fate, until we actually were within the towns perimeter.

In a few hours, when chemotherapy ends, we will have stepped, breathlessly into the glorious city limits of Remission.

Only then will we be able to exhale.

Epilogue

At the sound of his voice, I turn. "Hey, come feel this" my husband says, as I walk into the kitchen. I find my husband of 25 years with his hand in his pocket, nervously fidgeting. My blood immediately runs cold and a quiet voice screams out in the back of my mind, "No, no, not again. No more cancer. We only had five months in remission, this can't be happening again."

"It's not another lump, is it?" I ask, tears gathering in the corners of my eyes, my heart jack-hammering in my chest.

"No, it's not that," he says, a smile filling his face, a strange light gleaming in his eyes. "It's just that I was wondering, if you would be willing to spend the next 25 years with me?" he says, as he pulls a small, jewelry box from his pants pocket.

"Happy Anniversary"